PRAISE FO
BERLIN ALEXANDI

'A raging cataract of a novel, one that
threatens to engulf the reader in a tumult of
sensation. It has long been considered the
behemoth of German literary modernism,
the counterpart to *Ulysses*.'
NEW YORKER

'[An] immense and splendidly gritty novel…
funny, shockingly violent, absurd, strangely
tender and memorably peopled.'
PARIS REVIEW

'Döblin is never sentimental, or hysterical.
He just gets us to listen to the drumbeat of
violence throbbing in this city of the mind…
One of the great anti-war novels of our time.'
AUSTRALIAN BOOK REVIEW

'I learned more about the essence of the
epic from Döblin than from anyone else. His
epic writing and even his theory about the epic
strongly influenced my own dramatic art.'
BERTOLT BRECHT

ALFRED DÖBLIN (1878–1957) was a German novelist, essayist and short-story writer. He was also a doctor, practising psychiatry in working-class Berlin, the setting of both his most famous novel, *Berlin Alexanderplatz*, and his true-crime tale *Two Women and a Poisoning*. In 1933 Döblin was forced to flee Germany because of his Jewish origins, and he lived in France and the USA for the duration of the war.

IMOGEN TAYLOR is a translator who has lived in Berlin since 2001. Her translations include *Promise Me You'll Shoot Yourself* by Florian Huber, *Fear* by Dirk Kurbjuweit and *The Truth and Other Lies* by Sascha Arango.

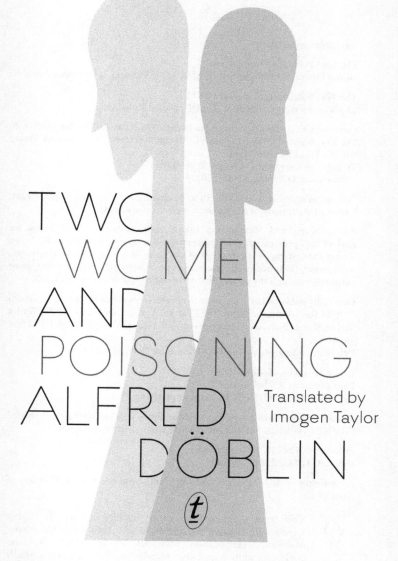

TWO WOMEN AND A POISONING

ALFRED DÖBLIN

Translated by
Imogen Taylor

TEXT PUBLISHING MELBOURNE AUSTRALIA

textpublishing.com.au

The Text Publishing Company
Swann House, 22 William Street, Melbourne Victoria 3000, Australia

The Text Publishing Company (UK) Ltd
130 Wood Street, London EC2V 6DL, United Kingdom

Copyright © 1924 Die Schmiede, Berlin. 1992 Patmos Verlag GmbH & Co. KG, Walter Verlag, Düsseldorf. All rights reserved by S. Fischer Verlag GmbH, Frankfurt am Main.
Translation copyright © Imogen Taylor, 2021
Introduction © Imogen Taylor, 2021

The moral rights of Alfred Döblin to be identified as the author and Imogen Taylor as the translator of this work have been asserted.

All rights reserved. Without limiting the rights under copyright above, no part of this publication shall be reproduced, stored in or introduced into a retrieval system, or transmitted in any form or by any means (electronic, mechanical, photocopying, recording or otherwise), without the prior permission of both the copyright owner and the publisher of this book.

Originally published in German as *Die beiden Freundinnen und ihr Giftmord* © 1924 Die Schmiede, Berlin. 1992 Patmos Verlag GmbH & Co. KG, Walter Verlag, Düsseldorf. All rights reserved by S. Fischer Verlag GmbH, Frankfurt am Main.
Published in English by The Text Publishing Company, 2021

Cover design by Chong W.H.
Page design by Rachel Aitken
Typeset in Sabon 11.5/17.5 by J&M Typesetting

Printed and bound in Australia by Griffin Press, part of Ovato, an accredited ISO/NZS 14001:2004 Environmental Management System printer.

ISBN: 9781922330383 (paperback)
ISBN: 9781925923803 (ebook)

A catalogue record for this book is available from the National Library of Australia.

This book is printed on paper certified against the Forest Stewardship Council® Standards. Griffin Press holds FSC chain-of-custody certification SGS-COC-005088. FSC promotes environmentally responsible, socially beneficial and economically viable management of the world's forests.

CONTENTS

INTRODUCTION

Alfred Döblin is a major writer's major writer. Though renowned as the author of that great feat of literary modernism, *Berlin Alexanderplatz*, his name rarely makes it to best-of lists, even in his native Germany. But his fan club is impressive: Bertolt Brecht and Günter Grass named him as an important influence; Walter Benjamin compared him to Dickens; W.G. Sebald devoted an entire PhD thesis to his work. 'We have all learnt from you, or tried to,' Stefan Zweig said in a letter to Döblin.

Reading Döblin is an experience. 'He will unsettle you,' Grass wrote, 'he will trouble your dreams, he will stick in your throat...Complacent people should beware of Döblin.' That is as true of his true-crime story *Two Women and a Poisoning* as it is of *Berlin Alexanderplatz*. Though stylistically less adventurous than the later novel, *Two Women* does not have the 'neatly ironed creases' Döblin disparagingly attributed to Thomas Mann's prose, nor does Döblin iron out the sometimes distressing subject matter—he has no qualms about wrenching us out of our comfort zone. Rainer Werner Fassbinder, the film director who made *Berlin Alexanderplatz* into a cult TV series in 1980, described his own experience of reading Döblin as 'dangerously often not actually reading at all, but more like living, suffering, despair and fear.' Döblin's writing is intense and at times relentless, but it takes us somewhere; it does something to us.

.

In March 1923 a trial was held in Berlin that caused a stir in the press and drew crowds of spectators. Parts of the evidence were so disturbing that they had to be heard in camera, but that didn't stop the Berliners from thronging, and perhaps it encouraged them. Women, in particular, came to look—or, as one reporter put it, 'the female element prevailed', presumably fascinated by the all-female cast of defendants: twenty-two-year-old Ella Klein, accused of murdering her husband and plotting to murder her lover's husband; twenty-five-year-old Margarete Nebbe, her lover, accused of aiding and abetting Ella and plotting to murder her own husband; and eighty-year-old Marie Riemer, Margarete's mother, accused of neglecting to report the murder plots.

There is no way of knowing what the 'female element' made of the case, but most of the (male) reporters were relentless in their defamation of the 'husband killers', labelling them 'unscrupulous', 'unfeeling', 'sadistic', 'abnormal' and 'inhuman', and deploring their sentences as shockingly lenient. The public prosecutor, for his part, declared them 'inferior female persons' with 'certain defects'. The disturbing evidence that had to be withheld from the public—namely Ella Klein's horrendous treatment at the hands of her husband—seemed largely forgotten by the end of the trial; what lingered was the image of a couple of man-hating imbeciles, or monsters, or both.

How different Döblin's account of the case. In *Two Women and a Poisoning*, he blends true crime and fiction, changing names and piecing the details of the trial into a story. But he doesn't use his novelist's freedom as an excuse to embellish. On the contrary: compared with many of the supposedly factual reports in the press, his slim text is a model of unexcitability and restraint. Take the opening sentences in which we are introduced to Elli:

> Pretty, blond Elli Link came to Berlin in 1918, aged nineteen years. Before that, she had apprenticed as a hairdresser in Braunschweig where her father was a carpenter. A childish impulse got the better of her: she took five marks from a customer's purse. She was sent to work in an ammunition factory for a few weeks and finished her apprenticeship in Wriezen. Elli was light-hearted and vivacious; it is said that her life in Wriezen was not ascetic and that she had a taste for carousing.

The language is pared down—no convoluted Germanic syntax, no high-handed narrator, little description. The sentences follow one another paratactically, with none of the paraphernalia of cause and effect; it is up to the reader to work out what goes on between them. Döblin gives us hardly more than the bare facts, the bones of a novel's opening lines, and it is a 'novel' that has neither heroine nor villain at its centre, but a pretty, skittish girl who likes a night out, an ordinary girl, a girl we have no reason not to like. Later in the book, when Döblin quotes an expert witness report that refers to Elli's 'infantilism', it comes as a shock. His Elli is often childish or childlike, but not pathologically so; we may not identify with her, but she is someone we feel we can almost understand. The clinical term puts a sudden distance between us and her that Döblin had been careful to eliminate. He treats the figures he writes about as people, not cases.

With the same care and respect, he slips a crime into this first paragraph so quietly that it barely registers—the faintest premonition of the murder to come. Elli is only just responsible. 'A childish impulse got the better of her.' The petty theft is something that comes over her, not something that she does, and the act is described not as *stealing*, but as *taking*. It is and is not theft, just as the murder that she goes on to commit both is and is not murder.

Döblin guides us discreetly through the intricacies of the case, offering limpid descriptions of the characters' confused states of mind and the subtle changes in their relationships to one another. He has a sharp eye for the quirks and contradictions of human nature, observing the fine line between sexual excitement and aversion in Elli, the strange mix of desire and inferiority complex in her husband Link, the compulsion that drives Elli and Margarete/Grete to exchange several letters a day, although they live in the same street, close enough to send curtain signals to tell each other whether their husbands are in or out. The book resists drama; the words 'tragedy' and 'tragic' appear only in quotation marks, spoken by others. And although Döblin mentions his forays into the places frequented by the two women—places very close to where he himself lived and worked—he does not stop to describe them, wary of resorting to 'tawdry social sketches'. The Links' flat is equipped only with a few select props, most of which we don't see until they go flying through the air during one of Link's tantrums: baskets of washing, plates of food, wicker chairs.

The text is altogether free of clutter. Döblin has a deep mistrust of language; vague and cumbersome, fraught with assumed meaning, it falls short of his scientific standards. Unlike the graphomaniac lovers, Elli and Grete, he prefers not to use too much of it, but to set things out as simply as possible; this approach is taken to its limits in the diagrams at the end of the book where the relationships between Elli, Grete and Link are presented in graphic form. Throughout his account of the case, he avoids explaining, interpreting, providing answers. He rarely judges. Only the chemist who sells Elli the rat biscuits and arsenic with which she will poison Link is described as acting 'very carelessly'—and the conventions of the trial are criticised as 'unreasonable' for demanding, almost *Alice-in-Wonderland*-like, that the jury ignore the bulk of the evidence that is put before them:

> The court asked no questions about the part played or 'blame' incurred by Link, Elli's father or Link's mother; it singled out one fact—the murder. Wrongdoing was permitted within certain limits; if they were transgressed, it was necessary to intervene. The jurors were urged to look away from what had happened inside the circle, within the limits; they were to ignore the wider gamut of circumstances. Really, it was unreasonable to show them the whole gamut and then expect them to ignore it. But a faint echo was all they were allowed to retain—enough to go on once the facts had been established and the time had come to ask: *And, are there mitigating circumstances?*

In a sense, *Two Women and a Poisoning* serves as a corrective to the failing of the judiciary; Döblin asks precisely those questions that were not put to the jury, and rather than home in on the murder, he turns his attention to that 'wider gamut'—the circumstances surrounding the crime, the subsidiary characters, the victim's role in his own death. He makes jurors of his readers and confronts them with questions that are murkier and more uncomfortable than the simple *did-she-didn't-she* of the court. This idea of leaving it to the reader to provide the answers is important to Döblin who, a decade earlier, in his 'Berlin Manifesto' of 1913, *To Novelists and Their Critics*, had demanded 'full autonomy' for the reader: 'he is to judge, not the author'.

The author, in Döblin, is not so much to blend into the background as to *be* the background, to *be* the series of events that make up a story, to pursue the process of self-denial with such fanaticism that he can say, 'I am not I, but the road, the streetlamp, such and such an incident, nothing more.' Döblin's term for this extreme form of authorial self-effacement is 'stone style'. His theories on literature are all about stripping things away, getting 'back to the concrete', casting off cliché, affectation, pointless flourish. 'Nothing superficial,' he writes in his open letter to Marinetti, 'no wrapping paper.' Figures of speech are put down as lazy and dangerous; the author, when he isn't a streetlamp, is a builder, dispassionately laying brick on brick.

In particular, Döblin is fiercely critical of any form of psychologising, railing against it as 'sheer abstract phantasmagoria...poetic gloss...dilettantish speculation, scholastic babble, whimsical bombast and flawed, fake lyricism.' Writers, he suggests, would do better to aim for 'factual imagination' and to learn from the more objective science of psychiatry which, rather than come up with contrived motives to explain a character's actions, only 'shrugs and shakes its head' at the hows and whys of a story. This is advice he himself will follow in *Two Women and a Poisoning*, never straying far from the facts, never falling into the trap of presuming he understands. The closest he comes to psychologising is in his interpretations of Elli's nightmares, though even here he is careful not to impose a single, unequivocal meaning on them, but to offer a reading that reflects the ambivalence and confusion of the dreams. It is here, too, that Freud's influence makes itself most clearly felt, and yet Döblin's interpretations have nothing of Freud's virtuoso but often far-fetched associations, with their heavy reliance on word play. He never forgets that he is trying to understand Elli; his readings of the dreams repeat the same simple words she has used in telling them.

If Döblin's account of Elli's poisoning of Link is what he calls 'factual imagination', his kind of imagination is closer to empathy than fancy; he even betrays a certain affection for 'cheeky little' Elli. Döblin the doctor is clearly present in the book alongside Döblin the author, but not just in the medical expertise he brings to the case. That is very much in evidence—in the detailed summaries of the doctors' reports, for example, and in the long list of symptoms suffered by Link when he begins to succumb to the arsenic. But the pastoral side of the job also makes itself felt— Döblin's concern for his characters, his capacity for listening.

Döblin always put a huge amount of research into his books, mugging up on Taoism and eighteenth-century Chinese history for *The Three Leaps of Wang Lun* (1915), machines and motors for *Wadzek's Battle with the Steam Turbine*, the Thirty Years' War for *Wallenstein* (1920), and everything from hydrography to seismology for *Mountains Oceans and Giants* (1924), a vast experimental sci-fi novel in which things spin out of control when Iceland is destroyed to melt Greenland's icecap.

Although a fraction the length of any of those novels, *Two Women and a Poisoning* was no exception: we don't know whether Döblin attended the trial, but he clearly had extensive knowledge of the various statements and documents read out in court. At the same time, though, the subject matter of *Two Women* was, quite literally, closer to home. Wagner Strasse, where Elli and Grete were both living when they met, was familiar territory to Döblin—and Elli and Grete themselves not only provided fascinating material for a doctor who specialised in 'nervous and mental conditions'; they were also from the same social milieu as most of his patients. ('It is rare that anyone from the upper classes strays into my surgery.') Five years later, working-class Berlin would reappear as the setting for Döblin's next and most famous novel *Berlin Alexanderplatz*. Like all his previous and subsequent books, *Two Women* has been somewhat eclipsed by that magnum opus, but there can be little doubt that it fed into it. As well as being set in the same social milieu, both works blend fact and fiction and make liberal use of newspaper articles to tell their stories; both are about a murder; both touch on the subject of female homosexuality.

Two Women started life as the opening book in a German series entitled *Outsiders of Society: The Crimes of Today*. Modelled on the French eighteenth-century true-crime collections of Pitaval, *Outsiders of Society* comprised literary responses to contemporary criminal cases; an ambitious thir-ty-two titles were planned altogether, including contributions by Thomas Mann and Joseph Roth. These would never be written. The series, perhaps a victim of the after-effects of hyperinflation, folded after just two years and fourteen publications. But Roth wrote an essay on the Klein-Nebbe case, which is included here, along with an essay by Robert Musil. Like Döblin, Roth and Musil rebel against the sensationalism surrounding the trial, and offer subtler, more sensitive readings of the case, shifting the blame from individual to society and, in the case of Roth, pointing up the absurdities of a social order where a woman 'would rather confess to murder than to a lesbian relationship'.

Times have changed. But Döblin's slim book remains compelling, and not just because of its subject matter. Other books have dated, become unreadable. Erich Wulffen's *Psychology of Poisoning*, a popular book from 1917 that perhaps contributed to contemporary interest in the trial, now reads as what it is—a heap of misogynist prejudices:

> Violent murder with its sharp and blunt
> weapons and its guns is not woman's way.
> She lacks the force, the personal courage,
> the determination, the skill. It is, you

might say, the soundlessness of poison, its discretion, that is suited to woman, its independence of physical strength. She sees no blood flow; what she does see— vomiting and pain—she is accustomed to seeing as the nurse of the family. [The] poison murderess assumes the duplicitous role of nurse to her victim and thus remains within the bounds of her sex's competence. The secrecy and cunning required to poison are often properties of female weakness; the female is also more capable of pretence than man.

Compare this with a passage from *Two Women*. So much is the same—the 'poison murderess' cum nurse, the duplicity, the feminine wiles. But where Wulffen's treatment of the subject is condescending and clichéd, Döblin's is nuanced and understanding:

Elli was confronted with the awful sight of her sick husband pacing feverishly up and down the sitting room, almost crawling up the walls with pain. She suffered cruelly. She took refuge in her letters, spurring herself on: I won't give up, I'll make him pay—even if I end up biting the dust myself.

Sometimes an animal indifference came over her. Things reached such a pitch that all tension suddenly gave way. When this happened, she would resignedly take him his invalid's gruel and 'finish him' while she was at it. She took a positive pleasure in obliging him to his face and tipping poison into his food behind his back. 'If only the swine would die soon...'

Unlike the cardboard cut-out that Wulffen calls 'woman', Elli is not only fiercely determined; she also shows signs of an almost sadistic schadenfreude that 'woman' presumably wouldn't be up to. At the same time, though, we see Elli suffer in her role as murderous nurse; we see her hinting at the possibility of her own death; we see her render sexual services to her victim with a cynical indifference that we know conceals deeper, more painful emotions. She is full of contradictions. She is real, human. We sympathise with her, in spite of ourselves. Döblin makes us see the black humour of the situation. And he shocks us into feeling and thinking.

TWO WOMEN AND A POISONING

Pretty, blond Elli Link came to Berlin in 1918, aged nineteen years. Before that, she had apprenticed as a hairdresser in Braunschweig where her father was a carpenter. A childish impulse got the better of her: she took five marks from a customer's purse. She was sent to work in an ammunition factory for a few weeks and finished her apprenticeship in Wriezen. Elli was light-hearted and vivacious; it is said that her life in Wriezen was not ascetic and that she had a taste for carousing.

She came to the Berlin borough of Friedrichsfelde. The hairdresser who employed her found her hard-working, honest, a woman of good character. He kept her on until she married, a year and a quarter later. He did not fail to notice her vivacity. It was on her nights out with a customer in November 1919 that she met Link, a young carpenter.

.

Elli had a special nature, though not a rare one. There was a naïve freshness about her; she was as blithe as a canary, as fun-loving as a child. She took pleasure in leading men on. Perhaps she yielded to one or other of them—out of curiosity, out of fascination for the other sex, or because she liked an innocent romp. She was surprised and amused at how seriously the men took it, how excited they grew. It struck her as funny. They came running along and you gave them a spin and sent them on their way. Then came Link, the young carpenter.

Link was dogged and earnest. He was an avid Communist and talked about political things Elli didn't understand. He fastened onto her, attracted by her shock of blond hair, her full, healthy cheeks, her cheerful outlook on life. She was sometimes so exuberant it made his heart swell. He wanted this woman as his wife. He wanted her at his side.

She saw nothing funny in that. Link was different from the men she was used to. He worked in the same profession as her father; she understood him when he talked shop. This somewhat constrained her behaviour. She couldn't play her usual little games. She felt pleased and honoured to be courted by him; she was in familiar waters. But at the same time, she was going to have to change; he had her in his grasp.

Elli sent home tentative reports: she had a good, steady position and was being wooed by a Mr Link, a hard-working carpenter with a decent income. This news earned her praise. Father and Mother were delighted. And, as Elli thought things over, she herself felt a certain pleasure. Really, she was quite fond of Link. He intended to provide for her, to let her keep house. It seemed to her that a marriage was something awfully droll, but nice. *He wants to provide for me*, she thought, *and he's pleased at the idea*. She really was quite fond of him. Still, she continued to have the occasional secret fling.

Link was in thrall to her. The longer they were together, the clearer this became to Elli. At first she thought nothing of it. All men were like that. But then it became irksome. It was so pronounced in him—so persistent. Almost imperceptibly, something took shape inside her; she began to resent him. Link prevented her from pursuing the fantasies she had begun to weave. She had fancied him a serious man, of the same stamp as her father; she had hoped to raise a family with him. Now he sank to the level of her previous lovers—no, lower still, because he hung on to her so, clung to her with such awful tenacity. Annoyed and pained, she realised that you *could* play games with him. He positively invited it.

She stayed with him. Things were already running their course. But the more time passed, the more aggrieved she felt. It was galling. Link had put on a front; she'd seen herself rising in the world. Now she was ashamed, not least of herself. It was a hideous disappointment.

This came out in occasional fits of rage. She was often not nice to him, rounding on him fiercely, shouting at him as if he were a dog. He was appalled. *She wants rid of me*, he thought.

She brushed things aside. He wants to marry me—why not? The prospect of keeping house was not to be sniffed at. And then he was so pitiful; she felt sorry for the man. She'd manage him somehow. She spent hours happily fantasising about married life. She would be a wife, with a family like her own. Her husband had a good position, he loved her, he was a serious man. They married in November 1920. She was twenty-one and he was twenty-eight.

•

They went to live with Link's mother. Elli was given no hand in the housekeeping. Her mother-in-law had said she would move out, but she didn't. She was not very kind to her son and he didn't much care for her. She wouldn't budge an inch to accommodate her young daughter-in-law. Every time they quarrelled, Link took his wife's side, deferring to her and hurling abuse at his mother. Young Elli listened, afraid that he might one day treat her like that. When she told him this, he grumbled at her. *What are you on about?* His income began to dwindle and he allowed her to take hairdressing customers. That strengthened her position against her mother-in-law. Now Elli kept house and managed the finances during the week. The old woman was allowed to step into the breach on Saturdays and Sundays, when Elli helped out in the business.

Then came a time when Link began to go out a great deal in the evenings. Soon he was going out alone every evening, leaving his young wife at home. She felt neglected. She complained that there was no pleasing him. He had rushed her into marriage. What had gone wrong?

He had grown up with his mother in an atmosphere of hard work and peevishness. He was keen to better himself. His fun-loving, tousle-headed wife had no fellow feeling with him; she remained as wayward as ever, following her whims, chopping and changing. One moment she clung to him, the next it was as if he didn't exist. Who is this man? she asked herself. He was a coarse fellow, fond of calling himself a workhorse. Now, wanting to possess her entirely, he drew closer to her—physically.

She had been involved with plenty of men in the past, but here was a man thrusting himself on her, who couldn't be shaken off with a laugh or a gesture of exasperation when things got too much. Here was a man making demands on her, a man who could claim a husband's rights. The physical contact distressed her. She suffered it in silence; there was something unpleasantly exciting about it. She forced herself to suffer her husband because she knew it was part of being married, but she would have preferred it if that particular part hadn't existed. She was always glad when she was once more lying alone.

Link had married a sweet young woman. He had thought himself lucky to have found her. Now he was cursing himself. What was this nonsense? She took her childish games too far; she wasn't good to him. He could be as nice as he liked to her during the day—and she was often bad enough then—but at night, in his embrace, she was dead. He resented her. She wasn't changing; now he had no home. He could treat her as tenderly as a doll, but when he tried to unite himself with her in order to win her entirely, she remained aloof, wouldn't let him near her.

She sensed his unease and it gave her pleasure. A gloating pleasure. He should just leave her alone. The next moment, she would try to be a wife to him again, to change the way she felt. But she couldn't. She realised anxiously that she was out of her depth. The thought flitted through her mind; more than once it drove her to yield to him. But her reluctance—that *I don't want to*—was growing stronger, and she felt a vast sense of revulsion.

In the evenings he escaped to his meetings—the more active and radical the better. The old sense of unworthiness reared its head. *I'm not good enough for her*, he told himself. *She's putting on airs*. He worried away at the thought. At other times, trembling with emotion, he determined to get the better of her. He was profoundly shaken by her sexual aversion.

.

Now when they faced one another, their positions had changed. He was disappointed, cheated of his expectations. Elli gave this violent and deeply divided man no joy, no fresh, new impetus; she withheld from him the warm, nurturing love she had shown him in earlier days—the love for which he had courted her. It was a disappointment similar to hers when she realised: *This is not the serious man I want to follow.* He shouted and made scenes in an attempt to shake it off. Then he began to fight. The matter was vital to him. He would not give Elli up. At first he took advantage of the situation to settle old scores: he lost all restraint, raged over nothing. His vengefulness was something of a boon to him; it almost reconciled him to her. This was in the first half of 1921. They had been married only a few months. He wanted to keep the nice, fun-loving girl he had married; she still had her old ways, her charm that reminded him of better times. He wanted to hang on to that. He wanted to hang on to her. He wanted to love her. He fell into bad ways.

Without knowing how or why, and with considerable inner resistance, he began to indulge in rough sexual treatment of her. To make violent, wild, extreme demands. There was a jolt in their relations; something shifted inside him. He couldn't resist the foul impulse. It wasn't until later that he realised he was treating her like a flirt, only more fiercely, more passionately. He was trying to hide his troubles behind his wild behaviour. He was trying to punish Elli, to degrade her in the very province in which she eluded him. She didn't like it—so much the better: her reluctance aroused him, heightened the thrill. He wanted anger. And deep down inside him, another emotion was stirring: by coming to her with his old reviled ways, he was subjugating himself to her all over again. He was exposing himself to her, seeking her approval. He wanted her to approve him, to *im*prove him. If not one way, then the other.

She understood, read the signs right. She was already used to going along with a certain amount to punish herself for her sexual inadequacy; there were times when she wasn't comforted by the all-consuming feeling of revulsion that made her husband seem unclean, gave him a bad smell. Now, although repelled and even afraid, she sensed that he was changing and wouldn't, in spite of everything, loose his grasp on her—that he was, once again, the old, supplicant lover, subjugating himself to her in a new way. She sensed that between all the ranting and raging and beating, he was once more yielding submission to her. And although she couldn't devote herself to him body and soul, this suited her better. When he came to her now, she felt an anxious but not unpleasurable excitement. She was pleased that he came and pleased that he suffered because he couldn't have her. It was, as it were, a continuation of their quarrel, their way of bringing the fight to a conclusion. It was more brawl than embrace. Gone was the sweet, pitiful, foolish behaviour of the past, the unmanly whisperings. He had opened up new territory inside her.

And so a quivering peace was made between them. He was led home in a new way and bound to her, as he wished to be. He had refused to give her up—and she had been swept along by him. There was no denying they had grown closer. But it was a path beset by dangers.

It didn't stop at fierce embraces. Husband and wife continued to change. Their wild behaviour flickered on into the day. They both grew more unbalanced and more in need of balance. They grew increasingly bad-tempered, irritable, fraught. She kept a beady eye on him, watching and waiting to see what he would do next.

He was filled with a feverish desire to let himself go. He raged in her presence, ripped clothes to shreds, tipped baskets of washing on the floor, all the time conscious of the pleasure it gave him. Best she saw him the way he was. He exposed himself more and more, telling himself in answer to his self-reproach that she must be punished, that he was master in his own house. He had wanted to start a new life with Elli; now there were times when he realised with disappointment that he was falling back into his old habits, powerless to stop himself. Sometimes he was seized with panic, filled with misery at himself, at Elli, at the state of his marriage. Distressed at the course things had taken. It was better when he wasn't at home. In those months halfway through the first year of their marriage, he spent almost all his evenings in public houses, cramming his head with radical political ideas. He took to drink. In inebriation he recovered his old freedom and peace of mind; he wasn't always longing for other things. He'd go home drunk and there was his wife. She had to submit to him—with or without beatings. And all was well.

·

As these changes took place in him, Elli grew quieter. She felt outmanoeuvred. Was she not, in fact, already defeated? Hatred stirred in her. Link began to beat her more often. They were sometimes up arguing until three in the morning and their quarrels were no longer subliminal embraces. Their wildness had almost entirely lost its old seductive purpose and given way to sheer brutality. And when he fell on her, the sexual, too, was bereft of emotion; Elli felt nothing but awful revulsion, swelling outrage and hatred. Elli, who had skipped into marriage with a smile and a sneer, had met with a brutal master.

They were still in Link's mother's flat and the old woman took a gleeful interest in developments. Link no longer sided with Elli; his mother was turning him against his young wife.

Elli was consumed with anger. She wanted to get away from Link. When she told him so in one of their daily arguments, he scornfully threw her trunk at her feet. But if she was angry at Link, she was angrier still at his stirrer of a mother. Elli warned that something would happen if things didn't change soon. Her mother-in-law felt guilty—she was afraid of the girl. Once she drank a cup of coffee Elli gave her. She thought it smelt sharp and acrid, and when she tried it with the tip of her tongue, it stung unpleasantly. You're trying to poison me! she flung at her daughter-in-law.

Elli tried the coffee herself and shrugged. You can live to be a hundred with me. The old woman told her neighbours about it; she told her son, who grew very sombre.

But now Elli changed tack. In June 1921, not

long after the coffee incident, she left the flat in Berlin and went to her parents' house in Braunschweig. In a fit of vindictiveness, she took with her all the money she could lay hands on—even what her husband had got for selling his bicycle, even the coppers from the gas meter.

·

Elli was in Braunschweig for a fortnight. She explained the domestic situation as best she could and her simple, petty bourgeois parents shook their heads. They didn't dwell on the subject. They thought she was exaggerating; she should calm down and stop being so childish. Elli herself was anxious to leave the horrors behind. She tried, with near violence, to resume life in her old surroundings. Her parents wouldn't own that she was right, but then, she was used to yielding to their calm opinions.

Her crabby husband, meanwhile, was left alone in the flat in Friedrichsfelde, listening to his mother grousing on about his bad, runaway wife. He roared at her, furious with her, furious with Elli, distressed with himself. But no amount of shouting could soften the blow he had been dealt; he was deeply sobered. Letters from him arrived in Braunschweig. In one of them, Elli thought she detected the voice of her mother-in-law. There had been terrible arguments in Berlin over that cup of coffee; now Link brought it up again: 'You must promise you won't do that to Mother, then everything will change.' He wrote in tentative, vaguely conciliatory tones. Her parents urged her to go back—he was waiting for her. She was beginning to feel freer. Her father was glad when, very reluctantly, she left, eager to please her parents. Her mother couldn't quite reconcile herself to the look of hesitation, the strained expression on her daughter's usually sunny face.

And no sooner were they together in Berlin than all hell broke loose again. It was as if they picked up their exchange where they had left off. Realising, almost as soon as they saw each other, that nothing had changed between them, they rushed headlong into their old quarrels. Now, though, Link had additional grievances to cover up and make good: anger at Elli for running away, humiliation at being left, shame at having fetched her back. Elli stood up to him, but before long she was quivering, suffering. Her parents hadn't wanted to keep her. Her husband beat her and she was no physical match for him. She couldn't face the endless, painful struggle. She felt that she was becoming a stranger to herself. She thought of the past, of all that had happened to her, of her life at home in Braunschweig. She thought of the person she had been at home and in Wriezen, and of the person she had become since. She sat there helpless, listless and sick of herself one moment, capable of anything the next.

He noticed her hostility. It gave him a jolt. He was shaken, called back to himself. He berated her. Why was she crying? It was her own fault. He went about feeling resentful and guilty, sometimes struggling with his old tenderness. Something had to happen. Something had to change. He acted on the resolve he had made in Elli's absence and arranged for them to move, to leave his mother's flat. *We'll move away from Mother*, he thought. *That will help.*

In early August 1921, they took a furnished flat in W. Strasse let by a Mrs E. They also began to go out together sometimes. On 14 August, Link took Elli along with him to Mr E.'s public house, the Hunting Lodge, to see a man he'd met not long before. This man was a railway guard called Bende. Like Link, he had brought his wife along with him. Margarete, she was called. Grete.

She was twenty-five, three years older than Elli, with sharply cut, almost severe features, brown eyes, a tall, rather bony figure. She sat beside her husband, a former sergeant, a stalwart, strapping man. He wasn't gloomy and troubled like Link, wasn't after Margarete as Link was after Elli. He had ways of his own. He was brisk and adroit, a man who had his wife under his thumb and liked to indulge himself. Margarete Bende was more reserved than Elli. There was nothing light-hearted or vivacious about *her*. She lived with her mother, to whom she was much attached. During the war she had become engaged to Bende, rapturous at joining herself to him. 'O blessed hours, o sweet felicity,' she wrote to her dear Willi at the front in September 1917. 'When, oh when, will you come back to me?' She signed herself his devoted Grete. In May 1918 they had married. The marriage had been very unsettled. It was hard for Margarete to prevail against her husband. If it hadn't been for her mother, she would have been pushed right into the background.

Elli was looking about her at that time. She needed something to lean on.

The women talked. While their husbands drank and made coarse jokes, they looked at one another, probing each other with their eyes. Margarete saw Elli's distress, but more than that, she saw her child-like manner, her slight figure, her shock of blond hair. They left together. They both lived in W. Strasse and arranged to meet. In the Bendes' flat Elli also met Margarete's mother, Mrs Schnürer, a kindly elderly woman with blue eyes. In the Bendes' flat they grew closer.

Mother and daughter noticed that Elli liked visiting them. And Elli saw that the two women held together against Bende. Mrs Schnürer was a calm, maternal woman and Grete good to Elli in a warm, affectionate way. For a short while, they sounded each other out. Then, on both sides, there was a release, an unburdening. Haltingly, in fits and starts,

Elli told Margarete what she could and Margarete listened feelingly. Elli had accomplished something: she was taken in, given protection. She didn't need to go to Braunschweig. It was a complete transformation, a liberation. She had rediscovered the old part of her soul, the good part—no longer screamed at or sat about helpless when Link raged, sure in the knowledge that she wouldn't challenge him. Soon she was seeing things as she had in the beginning: wasn't this the man who had fastened onto her, clung to her? Living under him, she had grown almost weak—no, loathsome. She pushed the shameful memories away. Cleaved instead to the image of Margarete, thought of her when she went home.

Grete Bende was a strange creature. She was given to vague, powerful emotions and loved fanciful, romantic turns of phrase. She understood little, knew that she often blundered; to refine and better herself, she spoke with a dark, swelling pathos. She had grown up with her mother and never left home; she was, even now, living with her mother. Grete's clinging devotion to her had left her dependent; she was brimming with emotions, but she and her mother between them had stifled her urge for autonomy. She made frequent attempts at freedom, but never in earnest; she remained the way she was, in a state of childhood. One such attempt was her marriage to Bende. That, too, had failed. She was too weak to keep a restless man like him at her side, let alone queen it over him with feminine wiles; she disappointed him in his desire to be reined in and dominated—provoked him to violence and arbitrary acts. Helpless and intensely jealous, she would escape back to her mother, who was always there, waiting for her. Grete felt hard done by; she was much given to protesting and complaining. The mass of frustrated feelings had surged and swollen inside her. And now here was Elli, playful little Elli, with her fun-loving, boyish ways, wanting help and someone to lean on. Grete was touched and moved and unsettled by her as by no one else before. No one had ever really courted this quiet, serious, rather gloomy woman. And as she wavered over what to do about her feelings for Elli, flattered, excited and charmed by the cheerful but troubled creature, Elli herself pointed the way. Grete must give comfort, approval, support. This loosened her ties to her mother; at the same time, Grete showed herself her mother's daughter by taking on her role. She drew Elli close. Elli was her solace, a substitute for the bad husband she couldn't hold on to. Answering some inner need, Grete hid herself, cocooned herself in her feelings for her. Elli

Link must be protected; she needed help. Grete Bende would give it to her. Elli was her child.

In this way they adapted themselves to one another. Grete released her dammed-up love on Elli. And Elli, freed of her burden and tenderly wooed, was relieved to find herself back in her old role. She was, once again, the cheeky little rascal she had been in the past, and Grete Bende was enchanted.

•

Link was shaken by Elli's escape to her parents. The raging continued, but he'd suffered a blow. His insecurity persisted after the move. He was flailing, groping; he had reached a turning point. Elli was changing her ways. But not enough and not for long— he could see that. And he too couldn't, no, *wouldn't* restrain himself; the ranting and raving had become almost mechanical. She could hardly hold it against him—that was his feeling on the matter. But it struck him that Elli's voice now had a slightly challenging tone when they argued, a strange, new edge. In some way, he realised—and this riled him all the more— she wasn't playing the game. When they quarrelled, she fought with incredible doggedness. That goaded him yet further. He resisted, objected: they had their own flat, he was earning a good salary—why weren't things getting better?

Grete Bende had been waging a more or less hopeless battle against her husband, notching up defeats. Now, yielding, overwhelmed, she took the battle beyond the walls of her house. She was fighting a bad man—Link. In her mind, he became almost as one with Bende. But she fought Link the more fiercely because there was a trophy, an as-yet unnamed trophy, to be won from him. Grete could take her revenge on her husband while, at the same time— and the thought stirred her tremendously—drawing close to Elli, undisturbed, a living being, a creature of her own, her very own. She could love.

Elli carried her rage to Grete, hot from the battle, and Grete received it with delight. Link fought, flailed around, struggled on. He didn't notice that he was fighting two people—or one new, fiercely strong person. Elli now had a second force of will—Grete— and that force was hard to contend with because he had no immediate contact with it, but could only take it on in the abstract, quite vaguely, in a kind of vacuum.

The two friends drew closer together. Grete drew them together. The woman couldn't let go of Elli. She burned to have a hand in every aspect of her marriage. It was a sign of her insecurity and impetuousness that she was unable to stop telling Elli what to do. Jealous and sensitive to anything and everything, she had to give her instructions. Grete was oddly troubled in those early days by the strange, though understandable, force of Elli's resistance to her. Elli hated her husband, but not as keenly as Grete would have liked. Elli chopped and changed—and Grete with her. One day Elli would come to her, agitated, weepy, bursting with anger, and Grete would talk to her soothingly; they would sit cosily side by side. The next day Elli would be a dear, but she wouldn't say a word about Link. Nor would she listen to Grete's scornful remarks, her usual rants. This made Grete unspeakably sad. She often talked about it to her mother—but kept from her what she felt. Elli, poor child, must be freed from that bad man, that scoundrel who beat her and didn't deserve such a woman. She let him run rings around her. Grete's voice trembled with indignation as she spoke.

She pushed herself closer to Elli. A correspondence—a strange correspondence—began between the two of them, two women who lived in the same street, saw each other daily and yet felt the need to prolong their conversation, their advances and rebuffs, even into their brief periods of separation. They wrote as lover and beloved, pursuer and pursued.

At first, they didn't write much. Then they discovered the lure of writing, the peculiar thrill of keeping up the game of friendship, pursuit and love when the other was absent. There was something strangely stirring about it, something sweetly secretive—and half consciously, half unconsciously, they continued in their letters along the courses they had set themselves: Grete was the pursuer, luring Elli, catching her, taking her husband's place, while Elli was given to playfulness, surrender, protests of submission. The letters seem to have been a means of helping one another, of plotting against their husbands, and soon, more than anything, they were a form of self-intoxication. They wrote to spur each other on, to reassure one another, outshine one another. The letters were an important step on the path to further secrecy.

Grete's mother stood by the two women. Elli treated her with affection and flattery. Before long she was calling Mrs Schnürer her second mother. Like Grete, Mrs Schnürer felt rejected by Bende; Grete was all she had and she saw how badly he treated her. She looked on, sharp-eyed and compassionate, as her daughter fought for her husband's attention— felt Grete's rejection as her own, drew her closer with maternal indignation. It was no mere negative feeling that moved her; she was reclaiming her daughter, who was everything to her. The circle widened and Elli stepped in—became her daughter's friend. Her fate resembled Grete's. The three women isolated themselves from the men, became warmly attached to one another. In spite of their different attitudes towards one another, they were a small community. They were at ease in their feelings, found a three-fold security in their rejection of the boorish men. In a letter to Elli, Grete Bende wrote: 'When I was standing at the window waiting for you yesterday evening after eight, Mother said to me: Look at those three tulips there, so close together. The three of us—you and Elli and I—must stick together like that, too, and we must fight until we've won.'

.

That was the state of play between them. Now Grete fell into a sweet fever brought on by Elli. Very gradually, very slowly, this fever aroused something similar in Elli herself. They had set off down the path of secrecy in mere defiance of their husbands; now they were propelled down it headlong. But neither admitted to the other—or to herself—that their path had veered off course.

The men were brutal; the women fended off their savage attacks. But in between times, Elli and

Grete listened to one another, tender, sympathetic. There was something in it of a mother swaddling her child. Elli was bright and playful, droll and flattering towards her friend. But passionate Grete, with her too-profuse emotions, spoke nice words to her and pressed her hand, making sure of her. Elli had to confess to herself that she'd never known such seductive tenderness. She hadn't expected to play more than the cheeky rascal and the little cajoler. Now, against her will and with a surprise that was far from pleasant, she felt herself touched and captured. To justify herself, Elli reminded herself of her husband's brutality, the whole reason for this friendship of hers. She was violently ashamed—though she couldn't have said why—of the secrets she shared with Grete Bende. This weakened her position against Link. It meant that she was sometimes cold towards Grete, without Grete's understanding why. At other times, she would turn her shame and guilt at her relations with Grete into exasperation and anger at her husband, concealing her guilt, now blindly, now with the dim sense that he was partly to blame—*if it wasn't for him, I'd never have come to this.* Each scene with Link threw her more forcefully into Grete's arms: this time she would stay with her; she was right to stay. Her feeling for her friend deepened and, polyp-like, spawned others.

Link worked, tried to placate his wife, shouted at her again, drank. He was in a rut and only digging himself deeper, though he did, at least, have his wife back. Her parents were on his side; she would sow her wild oats with him. He continued to attack her sexually; she suffered it with intense repulsion, making no attempt to conceal her loathing or disgust. She wanted to get right away—away from the region of her psyche that he had ripped open—a region of strife and savagery and tangled hatred.

Her mind was awhirl with the emotions aroused in her by Grete and Link. She went running to Grete for peace and quiet. She neglected her little household. When Link set her chores and errands in the mornings, she was in such turmoil—and so disinclined to think at all—that she forgot to do them. She had to note down his instructions, and when he saw this, he took more pleasure than ever in setting her tasks; it was his way of making her think of him during the day, of tying her down, cutting her to size. Then, in the evenings, when he came home, he could put her in her place. How afraid she was when he got back, usually drunk. How frenzied his rage. At such moments, the Elli who stood up to him didn't exist. He raged because he was master. These were the ruins, the relics of his great passion. He broke everything he could lay his hands on, making wild grabs for pieces of china, the table, wicker chairs, linen, clothes. 'Don't be so hard on me!' she would shout. 'I do my best. What do you expect of me? Stop hitting me over the head! You know I can't stand being hit over the head.'

He: 'Get your wits together!'

She: 'My God, you won't get anywhere talking to me in that tone. You'd do better to say something nice for a change. You make matters worse and worse, till I can't promise anything. You keep on till the measure overflows.'

He: 'You little silly! What can *you* do? Here's the rubber truncheon. That'll sort you out!'

How she hated the man. She wrote bitter letters to her parents. They'd driven her back to him; she wanted them to know how things stood. She told them she was making her husband feel as unwelcome as she could—let him leave if he didn't like it. She got him his grub and that was it. Just the sight of him made her want to spit, she hated him so much. All that mattered was that he kept working—earned his keep and hers. She was planning to run away from him again and take everything with her—the bed he'd bought, even his mother's allowance. There was no such thing as theft within marriage.

But even in the clutches of hatred—and hatred was something she willingly embraced—her words were bitterer than her feelings. She tried to justify her fondness for Grete, while refusing to admit it, either to herself or to anyone else; she spoke of their friendship in veiled terms. A strange conflict arose in Elli. She noticed it daily in her dealings with Grete; it became impossible to ignore. Elli told her about the goings-on with Link every day, but she felt forced into a role. She had to exaggerate and sometimes to put things in a false light; she had to deny the other side of her relations with her husband. She was leading a kind of double life. This toing and froing was not what she wanted.

Then things were settled, at least for the time being. Love flared up between the two women. From merely swearing friendship, comforting one another, kissing, hugging, sitting on each other's laps, they progressed to sexual acts. It was Grete—emotional, passionate Grete—who found herself making the first, quivering move. At first, Elli had been her child, in need of protection. Now Grete was full of admiration for the girl's resolve, her active energy. She pushed her firmly into the role of a man—a man who loved her and let her love him. She was not a woman who had ever been happy in the company of men, least of all that of her own husband. Now Elli was her man. Over and over she had to assure Grete that she loved her; Grete couldn't have enough of her protestations, her tokens of love. And Elli, who was pushing herself free of Link, allowed Grete to lead her down this path. Her active energy and manly resolve now had a sexual foundation and began to grow dangerously.

After these events, the women felt more secure, more convinced that they belonged together. They still felt some shame and guilt towards their husbands, but it was waning. Elli began to repel her husband more fiercely. What she said and wrote to Grete was the truth: she often refused her husband intercourse, suffering him only under compulsion.

·

At that time, towards the end of 1921, the Links often came to blows when they argued. Elli was consumed with hatred for her husband. He was the stronger; she ended up with bumps and minor head injuries. She had her injuries certified by medical counsellor Dr L.

During her talks with Grete, Elli had made up her mind to separate from Link. She and Grete—the pair of them by now in a state of near delirium—had more than once talked through their splendid plan: the three of them, Grete's mother, Grete herself and Elli, would all live together. The notion of divorce was firm in Elli's mind. Her only thought now was to be active and manly, and prove her love to her friend. She hardly so much as glanced at her husband. He worked through the night in the days leading up to Christmas—two thirty-four-hour stints—but she went running to Grete. Bende had banned Elli from the house; he didn't like the way the two of them sat around gossiping. Link didn't want Elli seeing Grete either. He didn't think much of his wife's visits to her, jealously suspecting that there was a man involved. The two women lived in fear of being caught by their husbands, often meeting only fleetingly on the street. Their emotionally inflammatory correspondence swelled; it had become an escape from their husbands, a manless utopia. They gave each other the letters in person on the street, only occasionally having them delivered. They had agreed on lace-curtain signals at their flat windows to communicate their husbands' presence or absence.

New Year's Eve was particularly bad. Link, bleak and dismal as ever, was again irritable to an extreme. They spent the day at his sister's house. When he and

Elli were alone for a moment he said menacingly: 'You dare to come home and you'll be gathering up your bones.' Frightened, Elli told Link's sister, who took Elli's side: if things didn't change, Elli would have to leave him; he'd just have to go back to Mother. She arranged for the couple to stay the night with her. On New Year's morning Elli went home. It was getting on for evening by the time Link got back, drunk. The shouting and name-calling started up—'you whore, you bitch'—the hits and blows.

On 2 January, Elli secretly ran away. She had discussed her preparations for escape with Grete and her mother, who had found her a room in the house of a Mrs D. Elli's right temple was bruised black and blue when she knocked at this woman's door. But she was free. Her husband didn't know the address.

Grete Bende was triumphant. It was as if, in her timid, hesitant way, she had escaped with Elli. She felt easier in herself; she was stronger, more assured in her domestic battles. Elli was all hers. She greeted her escape with enthusiasm. Elli must stand firm, they must stick together, strike while the iron was hot. 'But my love, if you go back or love anyone else, we shall be gone from your sight.' Knowing Elli's doubts and weaknesses—for she knew her own— she warned her against Link. He was a rogue and a scoundrel, and his letters were a mockery—pure infatuation; she mustn't be taken in by them. He deserved to perish in the gutter. 'One thing I swear to you, if you take up with that man again, I am lost to you forever.' Grete saw with apprehension that Elli had fled like a hunted woman—and only with her help. When she was calmer and Link began to woo her back, things would become dangerous. She wrote to Elli—for she was still writing, thrilling at the dreamlike atmosphere of the letters—and said that she and her mother had too great a sense of honour and too much character to darken Elli's door again if she returned to her husband. The thought was more than she could bear; her heart would collapse with grief and anguish.

Link was on his own. His mother wasn't in the flat with him. He drank, cursed to himself, went and ranted to her. Elli had behaved disgracefully again. She was ruthless. She'd get the better of him again, he could tell. He felt helpless fury at the thought that the silly little thing dared toy with him in such a way. Rebellion was useless. It only scratched the surface. He felt the opposite of rebellious. He was already defeated, trying to love her once more. In the first days of pain and vindictiveness, he resisted. Then he was his old self again, the man he'd been at the time of their engagement. He went over the scenes of the past days. He'd been awfully bad to little Elli. His old sense of inferiority stirred; he wanted to change his ways, and took this to mean that he was longing for her. With each day that she didn't come and he didn't hear from her, his longing and affliction grew stronger and his sense of unworthiness deepened. He talked to his landlady, who confirmed to him, when she saw his distress, that Elli was always rushing off to see her friend and neglecting the housekeeping. Link resisted for a few days longer; then he laid down his arms. He wrote to her parents in Braunschweig, glad to feel the paper beneath his fingers and to know that the conversation with Elli was beginning. 'How often,' he wrote deploringly, 'have I asked my dear wife—asked and asked her—to speak to me when I come home? How often have I told her not to spend all day at the Bendes'?' And then: 'Surely, too, it isn't hard to see why I hit Elli. Just think, I'd worked long hours to give my wife a nice restful Christmas and get ahead a bit, and when I come home after work like that, I'm worn out in body and mind. Elli says she's going shopping and then goes to see her friend instead, against my wishes and those of Mr Bende. She refuses to leave, though Mr Bende has forbidden her the house. The Bendes get into a row. Why must Elli do it? She hit me in the face and got a few slaps from me and all.' He ended the letter with long protestations of love.

Not far away, in Mrs D.'s house, his wife felt

calmer, glad to be in Grete's hands. She hadn't gone to her parents' this time. Her friend was close by; all was plain and clear. She went to see a lawyer, Dr S., and told him of the maltreatment. The lawyer applied for a temporary injunction that would permit her to live apart from her husband and charge him with paying her a monthly allowance and advance court costs. The medical certificate and a statutory declaration from Mrs Bende and her mother were presented as substantiation. On 19 January the temporary injunction was granted without a hearing. Divorce proceedings were fixed for 9 February.

That was Elli's course of battle. She was all set to free herself, to sever her ties with Link. Things would have continued along this path. But a few houses down the road—tormented, full of self-reproach and morbidly unhappy—Link was steadying his nerves with beer and schnapps, and demanding his wife. His sense of urgency was such that he stopped writing letters and took it upon himself to travel by train to her parents in Braunschweig. He couldn't let her go. He was plunging headlong, unrestrained. Just as, previously, he had beaten his wife, drunk himself into a stupor, ripped things to shreds and smashed furniture, he now felt compelled to write letters and dash to the station. It wasn't an urge to improve anything or to change himself, but a bleak, unrestrained surrender. A grinding compulsion.

His in-laws were not welcoming. Elli's letters had upset them. Her mother was in two minds. Her father maintained his old patriarchal view: a woman belongs to her husband. He gave Link Elli's address. And when Link's beseeching, almost humble letters received cold, disdainful replies, Elli's father accompanied Link to Berlin.

The ring around Elli and Link was tightening. The two men saw to that. The only question was which of the pair would survive, Elli or Link.

On her own initiative—and urged on by Grete—Elli had set the process of separation in motion. But as she sat alone in her room or with her friend, she began to have second thoughts. And when her family became insistent and Link turned up with her father, those thoughts grew stronger. Elli was repelled by the terrible Link—by the bullying, the rape, the black moods—but she was beginning to feel trapped by Grete and her thirst for love. There were also things she missed. It seemed to her that Grete had less to offer than Link. She couldn't give her a home or social dignity, not to mention financial support or the normal sexual life which, in spite of everything, she had adapted to. She'd jumped out of the frying pan into the fire. That wasn't what she wanted. She had no desire to be tied to Grete, to give herself up to her so completely. Shame and guilt at their relations throbbed away in her constantly. It reached a climax when her father arrived.

What she really wanted was to flit around a bit, enjoy a not overly rigid marriage, and stay close to her father and mother. Although she'd gone her own way at an early age, she had never quite left the parental home, always remained the daughter. Her love of fun, too, was that of a maiden daughter who is dismissive, and even fearful, of all things sexual.

Her father was accompanied by Link. She had known he would come looking for her and that he'd do his damnedest to find her. Grete was right, he was a boorish scoundrel. Elli took pleasure in upbraiding him in front of her father. In these altercations, too, she showed herself her father's daughter; she was more than a match for the simple man from Braunschweig. Link was soft, admitted his guilt. Feeling triumphant—and giving vent to her hatred and vindictiveness—Elli continued to heap him with accusations of boorishness and depravity. She was of one mind with her father.

It wasn't long since she had run to the lawyer to petition for a divorce. Now she changed tack.

Her father remained firm: a woman belongs to her husband. Seeing her father was, once again, an event for her; he was her family, her home soil; she stooped to the well-spring and drank. She had worked off most of her recent agitation. She would and must obey her father. She had to. Now, more than ever, she was intimately bound up with him. It was he who had married her to Link. Link took on a new face. Elli's relations with Margarete emerged in a clearer and very disagreeable light. Watching and listening to her father, she was ashamed of her hateful male wildness. Link was tame; her parents were taking care of her: it might all end well. It *would* all end well.

Her father left. She promised him she would return to Link. But there remained within her—especially after her father's departure—a certain unease, a lingering doubt. There was something unsatisfactory about deciding to go back. Elli felt discontent as she relented; her fear and anxiety and misgivings vented themselves in scenes of strife. It was two days before she gave up her room at Mrs D.'s. For two days she remained undecided, torn. It was a relief to her when, on the third day, her husband flew into a rage and threatened her. She went back with him to their flat. She did as she was told. Father and husband had decided for her. She felt strangely little shame before Grete; her feelings for her friend had strangely faded over the last few days.

.

Once Link had her back, he felt better again. The compulsion had released its hold on him—or perhaps he was sated. His mind was at ease. He could sleep and work and laugh and be glad with her. What a good wife he had! And she respected him. She was ebullient. They walked arm in arm. Elli rarely thought of Grete. She thought she might let her go. These were days almost happier than the time of her engagement. Ten days. The two of them were deep in wilful obfuscation, an almost dreamlike state which was partly an act and couldn't be sustained.

It was little things that brought them to themselves and opened their eyes to each other. It began with the return of a certain tone of voice, with bouts of ill humour, petty squabbles. They both began to slide. Soon they were back on the well-worn path.

They had fallen back to earth. That was how it felt. They hadn't bettered themselves—only forgotten themselves. And what a fall. Everything in smithereens. Raging with disappointment, Elli stood there in awful fury and thought angrily of her father—but it wasn't her father she was thinking of now. She'd only just escaped and that husband of hers had fetched her back; divorce proceedings were already underway and he'd brought her back—for *this*. He too was angry and didn't see that he hadn't had the strength of will for reconciliation any more than she had. He was determined not to spare her in any way. She'd made him run after her and fetch her back by force. Now she must pay for it.

Link felt as if he'd recovered his freedom. Such was his confusion. But Elli too felt as if she were her own person again. Link let himself go. Let himself loose on his wife. Drinking gave him courage, impetus. The awful and destructive spirit that inhabited him—the spirit of disappointment and rejection—drove him again and again to beer and schnapps. At such times, he cast off all restraint. The woman must be brought to her knees, shown who was master. He was relentless, forcing her lower and lower. He plagued her like an insect. He tipped food into their bed. He threw punches at her and laid into her with rubber truncheons and walking sticks. He didn't do it for pleasure. He was an unhappy man. He did it compulsively—blindly destructive, bitterly distressed, wracked by torment. Sometimes, after these fits of rage—after beating and insulting her, ripping up clothes and bed linen—he would emerge tired and calm from his dark savage mood. Usually, though, he felt a vain struggle inside him. A dull urge for release. He often went for her with a knife. And afterwards, when she'd freed herself from him, begging and hitting and kicking—one night he even tried to throw her out of the window naked—afterwards, he would pace about, rage some more, then walk out of the room, and before long she would hear a rattling sound and he'd be hanging on the sitting-room door or the broom-cupboard door by a rope, already blue in the face. Horrified, she would cut the noose and lay him down, filled with loathing and disgust.

At about this time, the fate of Link's father, who had died by hanging, began to insinuate itself into his life with growing persistence. The further Link deteriorated, the more he fell prey to that old fate, the more he came to embody it. Even without his wife's efforts, Link was heading for death. He was a wreck. He began to show signs of epileptic degeneration.

His sexual urge was heightened. His attempts to humiliate his wife grew fiercer and more frequent. Once again he led her on, driving her into the dark sphere of hatred, arousing in her the urges that would later be so hideously turned against him. It was, ultimately, his own compulsive hatred that killed him.

He rooted around in her body, eking sensuality out of every fold of her skin. He felt the urge to devour her, literally, almost physically. It was no mere turn of phrase when he told her in these fits of gluttony that he had to have her faeces—to eat them, swallow them. This happened when he was drunk, but it also happened without alcohol. It was self-flagellation, submission, mortification, penance for his inferiority and depravity. But at the same time, it was an attempt to cure himself of his sense of inferiority—by eliminating ambiguity. Quite apart from that, there was his wild lust—a murderous rage, cloaked in brutish tenderness.

In the savage sphere of hatred he engendered, she was soon as one with him, although she continued to resist outwardly, trying to push things away. Wasn't he, she would ask, ashamed to treat her in such a way? 'You're my wife, aren't you?' was the cynical reply. 'Shouldn't have married a workhorse, if you don't like it.' She would withdraw into her shell and hide when he spoke like that. But she had drawn him into her shell with her.

What was to happen now? Elli had often begged her husband for a child. He told her that if she had one, he'd put it straight out on the ice or stick a needle in its skull. She was on her own. Overcoming the shame she felt towards Grete for going back to Link, she again threw herself at her friend. She was uneasy to begin with. But she needed Grete—to talk, to give vent to her feelings and she didn't know what else. Everything was churning away inside her. So much so that she was often muddled, didn't know where she was or what she was doing. She felt confused anger at having gone back to Link—and because he had broken his word to her and her father that he would live at peace with her. And she felt boundless, tumultuous hatred towards the man who had abused her father's authority and now said to her, tauntingly, when they argued: you won't get away from me again. There was a constant rankling in her mind, she later said; she couldn't fight it. The sphere of hatred overwhelmed her, sucking up all her energy. To punish Elli for her forgetfulness, her bickering, her sexual rejection, Link stopped her allowance. But he wouldn't let her go to work. For all he cared, he said, she could earn money from men.

•

When Link had turned up at Mrs D.'s, Grete Bende had worried for Elli. She was bitter when she heard the next day that Elli was already back at home, perhaps lying in Link's arms even as she fretted. They didn't see much of each other in the week that followed. Elli avoided Grete, and if they chanced to meet on the street, Elli would abandon her friend after a brief, awkward conversation, and Grete would hurry home to take up her beloved pen and complain about this hurtful treatment, 'when you alone know that I cling to you like a burr on a dress. Why must you make me feel it so keenly when you're getting along well with Link? I could cry every time, my love, when I think of the cheerful way you went off with him.' Grete's grief didn't last long. She took Elli back as a repentant sinner. She was piqued that Elli had treated her as she had. But her love was fierce.

Elli was distraught, confused, downcast. She clutched at her friend, certain of only one thing: she needed her, wanted her, had to have her *now*. Her one desperate thought was that she must punish her husband—cast off the insult and disgrace that he had inflicted on her and her father. There must be an end to Link. He had roused wild feelings in her. Elli suddenly loved her friend with a passion. She was surprised at herself. She loved Grete the way a fugitive loves his hiding place or his gun, and threw herself furiously, ominously into her love. At the same time, she clung to her friend to preserve herself from the worst, for she already had some notion of what her lust for revenge might prompt her to do, and wanted to wrap herself about in fierce love, to make herself deaf and blind. Elli was already using the mysterious, obfuscating words that she would later repeat tirelessly: she wanted to prove her love to Grete.

This ardent love for Grete that was stirring in Elli was not a strong impulse that had been lying dormant, but a passion engendered and created by these particular circumstances. They unearthed something that lay atrophied inside her, an old, run-down mechanism. As people drowning in a shipwreck will perform monstrous deeds that it is almost impossible to believe their own, Elli was for some time at the mercy of an ineluctable force that sprang up inside her. It was the terrible man she had taken into her being and now had to cast out again.

The two women stoked their feelings of love with a constantly replenished hatred of their husbands— or, more precisely, of Link, for Grete's hatred of her husband was a pale imitation of Elli's; it was all show. Their thoughts of hatred served to justify and conceal the unmentionable peculiarity of their love, which they themselves considered criminal and punishable. Elli found an especial strength and security in their conversations, embraces, caresses. She felt just as Grete had when she once wrote: 'It is a real tragedy that we should be saddled with such types and have to do ourselves such violence.' She felt peace and security in a particular zone of her psyche—a zone to which she banished herself to contend with her husband. It was a zone consistent with her self: dangerous thoughts of revenge were at work in her; she wanted to do secret, criminal things. Throwing herself at Grete Bende was the first real step into forbidden territory.

The idea came to Elli first: Link must take to his bed so that he'd see what a woman was worth. This was already a clear wish for murder, but Elli disguised that from herself. Consciously, she was not yet ready to do away with him. Consciously, she was still wondering: How can I make him change his ways? The two women were now very restless. Their husbands kept them apart; Link was more brutal than ever. The women didn't know what to do. They went to fortune tellers who made the usual vague intimations about the future. Elli toyed with the idea of divorce, but again abandoned it. Why? Because she was already pondering a different solution in her mind; she said she doubted she'd find a lawyer who would agree to divorce them. In her letters, she often expressed shame at having returned to Link and caused her friend such pain: 'But you alone, you alone shall see, I will show you—I will sacrifice everything, even if it costs me my life.'

•

In these weeks with Grete, clear-headed, sober-minded Elli entered a strange and fanciful state of romantic exhilaration. It was something like the mood that had bound her to Link for a fortnight, only much more so—first dreamlike and then delirious. There was a complete shift in her inner outlook, a change in her emotional timbre. This was the effect of two powerful forces at work inside her: her indomitable hatred of Link—a feeling she wanted to drive out—and her passionate love for Grete. Elli's love in particular raised her to heroic heights, drove her to manliness and heroism. 'I'll prove my love to you,' she insisted, over and over. The two extreme and closely coupled emotions fascinated her. She fell under the spell of this fascination; it was to be some time before she emerged. She was often in a state of rapture and in this state it seemed to her that she lived only for Grete: 'Cost what it will, my only wish is to be happy and absorbed in my love.' She wouldn't listen when Grete tried to blame herself: 'No, I lay no blame on you.' Meanwhile, that other emotion kept surfacing: 'I want revenge and nothing more.' On whom did she want to take revenge, whom did she mean to punish, why did her urge for vengeance assume such fantastical forms? By this time, it was no longer an individual she was attacking—no longer the real-life man, Link.

At first, the sphere of hatred he had created within her drew to it the most powerful forces in her psyche; it expanded of its own accord, growing, looking for objects to fix on. But her old, underlying emotions took up position against this sphere, this alien power that had been hammered into her. She'd been in a state of inner balance that hadn't been easy to establish. The hatred had destroyed this balance, knocked her off kilter. Now the fine play of static forces was disturbed and the mechanism was working hard to readjust, to return to its old, secure state. Elli had to push away the new, top-heavy load and seek to re-establish order in her inner forces. She felt this task to be all the more urgent, because the sphere of hatred seemed to her alien, wicked, dangerous and frightening—out to destroy her inner purity, her liberty, her virginity. For, in a sense, Elli was and always would be virginal. She was engaged in an act of purging; a mass of pus was collecting around the infectious foreign body within her. The subliminal will to act had already taken root inside her. It thrived on Elli's fascination, her dreamlike state. It needed them. They were ideal conditions for its growth. And Elli, who had been drifting for some time, let it happen—indeed, she rushed into it. It was as if she were taking refuge in a trance or sleep.

But it wasn't her dealings with Link that troubled her the most. It was her inner conflict—Grete Bende. Grete was no better than Link; Elli even felt obscurely that her friend and her husband were one of a kind. Grete cajoled and courted her as Link had done; they were disappointed ditherers, the pair of them, both thirsty for love. Violently, almost fearlessly, Elli cast out the conflict that had taken shape inside her. She didn't want either of them the way they were. Distraught, she sided with temptation even as she resisted it.

Elli was in a state of crisis. Her fate had caught up with her as Link's fate had caught up with him. Her life too was in danger. After a furious scene with Link she thought of running away or poisoning herself—after first giving him lysol.

·

Why did Elli choose poison over a swifter means of killing? The hatred inside her was immense; she had to retreat in order to assert herself. It wasn't only weakness and cowardice that made her choose the feminine method of murder. Link made repeated attempts to hang himself. How curious that she should always cut him down. She'd stand before him in horror—then cut the noose, lay him down, let him get on with his wretched life. It was also her filial instincts that played a part in her choice of method, for these remained strong even when she was near to delirium. She wanted to kill so that she could free herself from Link and return to her mother and father. Her husband's elimination must remain unnoticed. Elli's preference for poison was bound up with her regression to childish feelings and family loyalty. Then there was the bond of hatred that tied her to her husband. He had roused her to unite with him in hatred, and it was a hatred intent on killing but not on death. They had been killing each other all along; she wanted to keep him so that she could go on killing him. Even as she slowly poisoned him, she continued to cling to him. At the back of her mind, meanwhile, she was thinking in all sincerity: He'll change his ways. That was the unspoken, uncertain but often-felt thought she kept from Grete: I don't want to kill him at all, I only want to punish him; he'll change his ways. Over and above her sadistic love, she felt a fondness for Link that sprang from her sense of family: he was her husband, after all. And, as she kept silent towards Grete, bitter and contemptuous despite her passion, she was under no illusions about the nature of Grete's relations with Bende.

Elli often seemed changed and absent when she was with her friend; she would apologise, saying that she'd been pondering how to get hold of something. Her fear of 'not getting hold of anything' and not knowing how to go about it was making her sick. At other times, she was confused, but ecstatic: 'You'll see, my love, I will fight for you and I will succeed. I shall know no rest in the world. But I'll put him to rest.'

It was to be rat poison. For two-legged rats, she would later write. It was the most unobtrusive—and something one might manage to lay hands on.

Grete had followed these developments with fascination. Fearful at times, but always happy and always with a thrill of love, she watched her friend set off down this path. Her own marriage wasn't bad at this time; she was far too absorbed in Elli's affairs to take much notice of Bende. She listened in delight to Elli's plans. It was fine by her that the man should go—that scoundrel, who had almost snatched her friend from her a second time. But she begged Elli to be careful, so she wouldn't have to face years of innocent suffering. 'Mother and I will never forsake you, ever.' From now on, Elli, too, took little notice of her husband's brutishness. Her fascination left her impervious to external irritants; nothing got through to her anymore. All that was over. Elli had only one thought now—murder. Her mind was made up.

Elli Link went to Mr W., the chemist, and asked for poison to get rid of the rats in her flat. He sold her rat biscuits. Some time later she returned, asking him to please give her stronger poison—the biscuits hadn't worked. Very carelessly, he sold her two marks' worth of poison, ten to fifteen grams of arsenic. The decision to get rid of Link was firm in Elli's mind; it was a child of her psyche and she had carried it full-term. Now she had to go through the horrors of putting her resolve into practice. She had no idea what she was letting herself in for.

This was in the months of February and March 1922. It was easy at first. Maybe Elli did something to provoke it, maybe she simply let it happen. Link staggered home drunk one evening, threw his supper in her face and pushed her onto the bed, demanding mashed potatoes. It was in these that he received his first dose of poison. A second followed three days later. The man grew sick; gastric symptoms developed. He was laid up for eight days, then went back to work. After that he got worse and worse. The poison afflicted his entire organism. Elli saw that he was trying to sweat, but couldn't—'the stuff was stubborn'. All seemed to be going well. He was having trouble getting back on his feet, she was determined not to give up. But other things began to happen. Through the haze of her fascination, she dimly saw what she had done. One day, when Link was feeling better, he didn't come home and she was afraid he'd collapsed—afraid a doctor had pumped his stomach and discovered the poison. Grete started to drop bleak, troubling remarks: apparently a person could burst from poison. Elli believed her and was afraid. Sometimes she didn't know what to feel: she was filled with an awful restlessness, could walk as far as her legs would carry her. She asked Grete whether this was her guilty conscience.

Grete saw the state she was in. If only Elli had given the man all the poison at once and put an end to everything. Then there was the hideous fear of discovery. 'But my only love, do take care that it doesn't come to light afterwards. The scoundrels aren't worth that.'

When Grete's husband heard that Link was sick, he said jokingly: 'Wouldn't be surprised if old Elli hadn't slipped him something. She's always saying she'll pay him back some time.'

'In that case,' Grete retorted, 'the doctors wouldn't say it's flu that's gone to his chest.' But a neighbour, Mrs N., told Grete's mother she thought there was something fishy about Link's illness; she was sure Mrs Link had a hand in it.

Mrs Link was distraught, all gone to pieces. Wearily she nursed her husband. She rallied, she faded. And he lay there and wouldn't die. He was repellent to her in a new way—loathsome. A poisoned man. She saw what she was doing; he was a horror to her, a physical indictment. She nursed him, often going to great lengths to be especially nice to him. She had set herself a ghastly task. When, yet again, he recovered, she felt enervated. She would wait until the spring.

Grete's keen eye, her eagle eye, saw some of this. Was it not possible that Elli was in love with her husband? No, no, Elli replied aghast. What an idea. She was doing all this for Grete's sake. She had to defend herself for worrying about Link; if she was as concerned as all that, Grete pointed out, 'she needn't bother giving him the stuff'. Grete had a tendency to exaggerate in her talks with Elli. Once she found herself boasting that she too was going to poison her husband. This, in spite of the fact that she generally got along tolerably with Bende, and always clung to him and fought for his affection. She had no intention of poisoning him. Elli let her have a little arsenic. Appalled, Grete threw it away, giving Elli the wretched excuse that Bende would stop eating at home if he noticed—and besides, she would have no part in the 'victory' if it came out. On another occasion, competing with Elli—but also to reward her—she told her what trouble she'd almost got herself into. She had tried, she fibbed, to give Bende hydrochloric acid, but he'd noticed and forced her to eat some herself and now she felt so sick. Elli believed her. Much of what Grete said and did at this time was no more than impassioned mimicry. She spoke of the violence she did herself at home. She felt nothing for Bende, she said, but thought it better not to take action yet. People would find it funny if both fellows went at once.

·

Elli was confronted with the awful sight of her sick husband pacing feverishly up and down the sitting room, almost crawling up the walls with pain. She suffered cruelly. She took refuge in her letters, spurring herself on: *I won't give up, I'll make him pay—even if I end up biting the dust myself.* Sometimes an animal indifference came over her. Things reached such a pitch that all tension suddenly gave way. When this happened, she would resignedly take him his invalid's gruel and 'finish him' while she was at it. She took a positive pleasure in obliging him to his face and tipping poison into his food behind his back. 'If only the swine would die soon. He's a tough old swine though. Today I gave him drops, and plenty of them, and his heart suddenly started pounding like mad. He got me to make him compresses, but I put them under his arm instead of on his heart, and he didn't notice.'

These were rare moments of cynical respite. On other days she was beside herself with guilt and inner torment. She would lie before him, begging him to stay with her, promising to nurse him. At such times she was his wife again, the good daughter from Braunschweig, and he was the man given her by her father. Fear of punishment loomed: 'If Link finds out he's been poisoned, I am cruelly, mercilessly lost.'

How Elli chopped and changed in the words and letters she exchanged with Grete at this time. Although the active, more masculine of the two, she now sometimes fantasised herself almost into the role of Grete's bondwoman. 'When I am finished with Link,' she wrote between horrific reports on Link's condition, 'I hope I will have proved to you that it was all for you, my love, that I saw this through.' Once, when the talk and rumours and false fears were too much for Elli, she took what was left of the poison and threw it down the lavatory. Then she was at a loss what to do. Her determination to get rid of Link forced itself on her, did violence to her. She racked her brains to find a solution. 'Grete, see if you can't get hold of something. I could tear my hair out. Why did I have to be such a fool? Now it's all been for nothing. Please, get me something, Grete, please. I can't believe I'll ever be properly free of him, but I must—I will—get rid of him. I hate him too much.' And the women sat together and cried; they had overreached themselves. Suspicious Grete sensed an unspoken reproach in her friend's behaviour. Her heart ached, she wrote in one of her letters; she felt her guilt and feared for her love.

Elli went once more to the chemist. Was again given poison. By this time, the victim was laid up at home or running from one doctor to the next. The doctors diagnosed influenza. Link's fits of rage abated. But he remained grim and bad-tempered. Sometimes he vented his resentment at his wretched state on his wife. He was a work beast. If only he could get out, if only he could work. Sometimes, when he looked at Elli, he felt remorse. She sat beside him crying and he didn't know why. To the very end there was no brightening or warming in his soul. The poison attacked his stomach and bowels, producing severe catarrhal inflammations. Vomiting and cholera-like diarrhoea occurred, especially after the larger doses. He grew very pale and grey, with headaches, neuralgia, weakness all over his body, occasional attacks of angina, deliria, swoon-like fits.

The terrible days in late March before his end were days of intense strain for the women. Grete was, despite her fearfulness, the calmer of the two: she was far from the action and, more important, she felt a constant delight at the thought that something was being done for her. She and Elli were still reeling off the same old phrase: soon there would be no one to destroy their happiness. But they were often feverishly afraid. Over and over, Grete urged her friend to be calm, warning her that if she happened to be questioned, she should confess and feel no remorse. When Elli came to call earlier than usual one morning, Grete felt a shock of pleasure, thinking she was bringing a certain piece of news.

Elli seldom felt anything for Link. She had only one thought in her mind now: there must be an end to this. Sometimes she felt renewed hatred for her husband because things had gone on for too long. Often she conjured up—or felt stir within her— the sweet, heady sense of fascination, the soothing feeling it gave her to tell herself: I am doing this for my friend, proving my love to her after inflicting such pain on her by going back to Link. In those days after her return she had thrown herself into her love with near violence—as never before. Now her love sometimes quietly took second place to her inclination to put an end to everything. As her hatred for Link diminished, so too her affection dwindled. But there was no going back. She harboured obscurely voiced thoughts of dying, disguising them as ways of escaping punishment: 'If it comes to light and I have to pay for it, I'll do away with myself at once.' And in another letter: 'If it comes to light—and, for all I care, it can—then my days, like his, are numbered.'

•

Towards the end of March 1922, the poison ran out again and neither Elli nor Grete could bear the suffering, the dread, the fear and trepidation any longer. Grete agreed that Elli should take her husband to hospital. Elli's vigour was broken. Weak and grateful, she wrote to her friend, saying yes, she would do it; and her second marriage would be to her.

Link was taken to Lichtenberg Hospital on 1 April 1922 and died the same day, aged thirty.

A weight had fallen from Elli's heart. She had no real thought for Link. She acted grief-stricken, but felt happiness and relief. Why? Because she no longer needed to kill, because she'd recovered her old self, because her own sickness was coming to an end. Soon, she hoped, her soul's pendulum would be swinging steadily again. What had happened? Elli only felt dimly that an abundance of horror was gone. She didn't feel harshly towards her dead husband; he scarcely entered her mind. At moments, she even thought wistfully of him. In a letter to her parents she said that Link had kept his promise in the end; he had changed his ways. She spoke only good of him— to herself and others. Fortune had been kind to her;

she returned to her well-ordered, smoothly running world. The anxious strain of the past weeks gave way to joyful exuberance. Elli was in a state of confusion. She foresaw nothing.

As always, she kept some of her feelings from Grete and was all joy with her. Elli was already thinking about the future: she didn't want to get married just yet, but maybe later, if something cropped up—the chance to help out in a business and a man with a fat purse. 'I'm the merry young widow,' she said in delight, with no thought for Grete's feelings. 'I had so hoped to be free by Easter. I've nothing to wear—now I can buy myself something. If fortune smiles on you too, Mother won't recognise us when she comes to visit. We'll be the merry widows of Berlin.'

Grete Bende had lived through the past weeks in fear and trembling, impatient for the day of the funeral. In the matter of Link's murder, she saw herself as the receiver, as bad as the thief. She didn't attend the funeral, but her mother did. Grete felt the need to comfort Elli: 'He's an out-and-out scoundrel, that man. He doesn't deserve to find peace in the grave.' But in another letter that day she wrote: 'My love, I wonder whether you are thinking of me as he is lowered into the earth, for really I am more to blame than anyone. My face is burning as if on fire. It is twenty to four. Any minute now, if all goes according to plan, the great ceremony will begin and Mr Communist will go marching out of this world.'

Elli needed no encouragement. Bold and cynical, if not entirely honest, she boasted to Grete: 'Have carried out all my plans and proved my love to you—proved that my heart beat for you alone and that my love for Link was a pretence to the end. You sometimes thought I felt pity for him. No, my love. I'm only happy that I've done it—that I've stopped his foul, godless mouth for four marks.'

But more and more, Elli began to feel chilled and sobered. She told Grete's mother Mrs Schnürer about Link's illness—how keen he'd been to get back to work and how his newfound kindness to her had more than once made her cry. She often sat with a wistful look on her face. The fascination was fading. It wasn't that Elli feared punishment as Grete did, but that she was beginning to see things with awful clarity, to revert to her old state. Grete observed this with dismay, feeling that Elli was turning against her: 'You are a great puzzle to me. How I worry and reproach myself. Even when I'm with you, your attitude towards me is always forced, as if you were trying to tell me that it's my fault you did it.' Grete's distress was great. Once, at her wit's end, she said she blamed herself for everything: Elli didn't really love her; she could have begun a happy life with Link when she went back to him.

The widowed Elli roused herself from her confused grief and defended herself: 'Dear Grete, how can you say I'm upset about Link? Aren't I boisterous enough for you? If all this was forced and false, I wouldn't be in such good spirits. Believe me, there wasn't a fibre in me that was moved. I was quite cold and did everything with a cold heart and haven't the slightest regret. I am only glad to have found release.'

•

At about this time, Grete Bende, courting and competing for her friend, feigned activity and pretended that she too was planning to do away with her husband. Perhaps her mind was frenzied and delirious. She was harried by the pain and fear she felt for her friend. But for every step forward, she took two steps back. She consulted the wizened old clairvoyant Madame Feist, bought arsenic drops, told Elli she'd give them to Bende. She was extremely agitated, and her love for Elli was pushing her to do things that were not in her nature. She didn't hate Bende in the least and when she embraced Elli, she grieved and wept in spite of her desire; something in her still strained after her husband. She kept putting her friend off—'Wait for me, stay true to me; things here will take a little time'—all the while ecstatic at the thought of fetching Elli to live with her and her mother. Grete, warm-blooded, emotional Grete, was horrified when the pert summons came from Elli that she must be free for her by Whitsun. Dejectedly she read Elli's letter of enticement: what a lovely time she was having all alone, no longer at anyone's beck and call, no more need to make allowances or be anyone's poodle. Grete, too, now got a glimpse of Elli's child-like, callous side—of an Elli who was fun-loving and easy-going, but also ruthless. Grete was in a conflict, almost a crisis. It was something of a relief to her when disaster broke and all was discovered.

Link's doctors had wavered between influenza, malarial fever and methanol poisoning. The death certificate gave methanol poisoning as the cause of death. It was Link's mother, ill-disposed towards Elli, who set the stone rolling. Elli told her nothing of Link's illness until after his death when she said he'd died of alcohol poisoning. Old Mrs Link went to the police and denounced her daughter-in-law. Questionings followed. An autopsy was performed and parts of the corpse were sent to Dr Br., a chemist, to be analysed. The chemical analysis revealed no traces of methanol or any kind of medicine. It did reveal the presence of considerable quantities of arsenic, enough to kill several people. The court medical officers diagnosed chronic poisoning with unprecedentedly large amounts of arsenic.

A search of Elli Link's flat brought to light a pile of letters—Grete Bende's and a number of Elli's own that Grete had returned to her. Some of these were found in her mattress. Grete Bende was laid up when the storm broke. On 19 May, a month and a half after Link's death, his widow was arrested. Grete Bende's arrest followed on 26 May. There were also investigations against Mrs Schnürer.

The brief reports in the press caused a furore. Investigations went on for almost a year. The trial was held at the District Court in Berlin from 12 to 16 March 1923.

Elli Link pleaded guilty from the start. She was like a shy schoolgirl. But as the trial progressed, she was moved to defiance. Her hatred of her husband revived; she felt blameless, had only defended herself, done away with the villain.

Her friend was shaken, horribly frightened—and liberated. Her old conscience had her in its grip. She felt guilty towards Elli, too. In her odd, inhibited way, she felt guilty, but remained evasive, hiding behind hollow indignation. Even at the trial itself, she denied everything—a thin, transparent tissue of lies.

·

In custody, Elli came to her senses. The fascination was quite gone. It wasn't clear to her how things had come to this pass. 'How can I describe it?' she wrote while awaiting trial. 'It is still hazy to me, nothing but a dream.' She had no sense of danger. Her burning fury at Link had subsided, but a general numbness and bitterness lived on in her, even now that he was dead—a numb, bitter condemnation of him, a stubborn aversion which made her feel better. She clung fast to his brutality and wickedness, and felt spurred to action. Her parents in Braunschweig stirred themselves to help her. Elli's lack of concern is evident in her exasperation at her mother-in-law: not only had the woman reported her; she was now meddling with Elli's belongings and Link's paltry estate. Elli alerted the lawyer who had handled her divorce proceedings. Must she put up with this? In a letter written in late 1922, she reproached her parents and brothers and sisters for not looking after her things. All her possessions were gone; she could tear out every hair on her head, one by one. 'The old woman's looking for ways to lay the blame at my door, but if she says anything,

I shall speak out too because there is such a thing as going too far. Link had nothing but torn clothes. If the lawyers don't pull their weight, I can reckon with years. Oh, that woman. Why must she raise such heartless children? Maybe I'll go barefoot; the old bag might like that.' Elli goes on to report on the continued fine weather, the glorious air. 'For heaven's sake, don't go and get ill; I want you all hale and hearty when I next see you. Do please keep my things in order. I shall have to make arrangements; I've a lot of responsibilities. Fondest love, your daughter and sister Elli.'

It seemed to her that she had got quite free of Link—that she had liberated herself from him. But she hadn't recovered her equilibrium. Now that her passion and her fascinated hatred had passed—now that she was to be punished because of Link—she found herself doing battle with him again. She wasn't through with him yet. Deep inside her, something still cleaved to him. She dreamt a great deal in custody and her dreams were heavy ones. Some of them she wrote down.

'My husband and I were walking through a wood and came to a fenced-off pit. There were lions in the pit; the sight made our flesh creep. Link lost his temper and said: I'll throw you down in a second! No

84

sooner had he spoken than I was lying at the bottom. The lions pounced on me, but I stroked them and cuddled them and fed them my sandwiches. They did me no harm. While they were feeding, I climbed up the sides of the pit and jumped over the fence. Link was furious: You hussy, he said, you're still alive. There was a door that was not quite closed. I gave Link a shove and he went flying down. The lions ripped him to pieces and he lay there with them in a big pool of blood.'

'I was sitting in my room with a little girl, cuddling her and laughing and playing. I taught her some phrases to say when Link came home. When we saw him coming, we went to meet him and said: Good evening, Daddy, did you have a nice day? When the little girl managed a few words too, he said: The brat's just like you—and tearing the child away from me, he grabbed her by the legs and slammed her head down on the corner of the table.'

'Link bought a little dog. He wanted to train it to be a watchdog and took the stick and gave the creature a real thrashing. Just the sound of Link's voice made it scream. I couldn't look, and scolded him for beating it like that: "Goodness and kindness would get you a lot further." When Link didn't listen, I took the stick from him and hit him over the head with it so that he fell down dead.'

'There was a large room filled with dead bodies, which I was to wash and dress. But I was careless and knocked over a bench and all the bodies fell to the floor. Picking them up made my flesh creep; I wanted to hurry away and cry out. But though I ran, I didn't move from the spot and my cry stuck in my throat.'

'The day of the trial. My sentence was very harsh. I was racking my brains for the easiest way to put an end to things, when a wardress came along and said: I'll help you—and took a knife and cut my body in two.'

'I heard Mum calling and went to the window. Then I heard someone come into my cell, and whoever it was pulled me away from the window.'

'I had a person in my room who was quite cold—whether a she or a he I don't know; nor do I know whether the figure was dead or alive. I was so awfully sorry that the person was so cold and took some glowing coals from the stove and put them by the bed to warm the person. But all at once, everything burst into flames and I was beside myself, like a madwoman. I wonder who else knows that feeling, when you wake up and none of it is true.'

'A person stood in the room holding a bucket with a snake in it. This person showed the snake which way to crawl and it coiled itself round me and bit me in the throat.'

'I was looking at a white flag with a black eagle, and smoking a cigarette. Without meaning to, I burnt a hole in it. For this I was court-martialled and sentenced to life in a penitentiary. I was in such despair that I hanged myself.'

'We were practising catch with four balls that changed colour in the air. Then all of a sudden they turned into heads and gave me such looks that I was terrified. It made my flesh creep and I ran away. But try as I might, I couldn't move from the spot. So I called to Mum: Oh, do help me. But the words stuck in my throat. When I woke up I was drenched in sweat.'

'Out walking in the country. When we came to a mill, we went in and asked for a little flour, but the miller was so hard-hearted, he showed us the door. I flew into a rage at this, gave him a shove and he went flying into the mill wheel, where he was chopped into little pieces.'

'My husband had always meant to go and live abroad. His wish was granted and he took me with him. On the ship I was surprised by all I saw, and curious too. I asked so many questions that Link turned nasty and threw me overboard. Somebody saw him and I was rescued. But Link didn't like having me back; I was a nuisance to him. It upset me terribly that first he'd talked me into coming with him, and now he wanted rid of me. I gave him a shove and he toppled over into the water and didn't reappear. But I kept seeing him coming up behind me.'

'"Didn't you always promise you'd buy me a pair of shoes? Well, now you can."—"All right, I'll buy you a pair of clogs. They're good enough for you." I said no, thank you, in that case, I'd rather do without. For that "thank you" he hit me so hard over the head that I was knocked senseless. When I came to, we were on the tram. Link said: Are you done sulking? It was only then that I realised what had happened. I flew into a temper. As we were getting off the tram, I pushed him in front of it. He was instantly run over and lay there in little pieces in his blood.'

Sometimes in prison, as she dreamed or dozed, Elli saw objects and faces that swelled and grew to many times their size. It made her eyes hurt, she said; it gave her such feelings of anxiety and such palpitations that often she didn't know what to do. She caught herself wandering around in a dream. She dreaded the night. Cold rubbings helped, but they couldn't stop the nightmares.

Grete Bende, too, often had vivid dreams of her

husband. He'd threaten her with a knife or hatchet and she'd be gripped by a crushing fear. But she also had easier, pleasanter dreams of strolling across green meadows covered with flowers, or walking through crisp snow with her dog. She very often dreamt of her mother and cried in her sleep until the woman sharing her cell woke her. In some dreams, she saw her husband raging at her mother. At other times she dreamt that Mrs Link—her Elli—was standing before her in tears saying: 'Link's given me such a beating again.'

Elli was violently affected by events, by imprisonment, by her interrogations. It wasn't only that she came to her senses; there was also—this was evident in her dreams—a change in her. For the first time she saw clearly and fully what she had done; for the first time it came home to her that she had poisoned and killed Link. This change was brought about by the passing of her passionate fascination—and by the filial instincts and sense of family that court and prison had quickened in her and that now released a rush of social feelings. By day she went about things with apparent cheerfulness and calm, but at night and in her dreams she was the object of fierce, deep-seated bourgeois impulses. She was driven towards her parents, her mother; she heard her mum call and wanted to go to her, but someone pulled her away from the window of the cell. That someone was her crime, keeping her from her mother.

In vain she went over and over the fact: 'Link is dead; I killed him.' She couldn't reconcile herself to it. The murder was constantly re-enacted in her dreams; she kept on killing, driven by her filial instincts, and made attempt after attempt to justify herself. Elli's dreams were a perpetual battle: her accusatory filial instincts fought for unrestricted dominion, while the remaining forces in her resisted—partly with the salutary intention of avoiding inundation by such formidable and crippling powers. To justify herself, Elli conjured up a metaphorical fall into a lions' pit. In this metaphor she explained why she'd had Link torn to pieces by lions. She was walking with him through the forest (of their dreadful marriage), when they came to a fenced-off area, a forbidden place, a pit of unconcealed anger, hatred and perversion. Link tried to push her in, but failed. She got away; he died there. It was only right. She was defensive in the dream, speaking only of his perversion, not of hers.

She offered herself proof of Link's brutality, most poignantly in the dream where he grabbed the legs of the little girl who was to greet him and bashed her head against the corner of the table. But Elli's dreams also addressed more hidden things. She herself had been just such a child; she had seen a similarity to her father in Link and looked for a resemblance between the two men. She wanted to call Link father, to go to meet him like the girl in her dream. But he disappointed her, dreadfully. She charged him with trying to kill her, with attempting to kill the child in her. This was her covert way of turning to her parents for protection, appealing to them as witnesses, asking them to be good to her. She dreamt that Link threw her from a ship, that he hit her over the head. Another dream told of her disappointment in her relations with Link: having promised her shoes, he said that clogs were good enough for her. His sexual attacks returned in veiled form in the image of the snake that crawled towards her out of the bucket and bit her in the throat.

And she tried to make little of her own wrongdoing. All she'd done was smoke a cigarette and accidentally burn a hole in a white flag with a black eagle. That was her violation of the law.

She didn't want to have to bother herself with Link or the murder. She complained that she had to keep on murdering, keep on thinking about him, although he was dead and gone. Her room was filled with dead people; she was to wash and dress them.

She wanted to push them away and run off, but found herself rooted to the spot.

All this time, though, the sadism, the convulsive love-hate that Link had aroused in her, raged on in her dreams. Everything was strangely at odds in Elli: her desire to purge herself, to be a child again, to return to her parents, drove these fantasies into her head; but at the same time, the sadistic urge was suckling at them, gorging itself on them. Her flesh crawled and yet she couldn't tear herself away. She couldn't return to her parents over the barbed fence of her conscience, but she didn't want to persist in her hatred. In her indecision, she contemplated death as a means of escape; in one dream a prison wardress helped her, cutting her body through with a knife. In another she hanged herself, as her husband had sometimes tried to do. Elli also identified with Link in the dream of the navy war flag. He had been a sailor in the war and she punished herself by suffering his fate.

All these dreams were a form of self-punishment. Elli shuddered at them, but continued to inflict them on herself.

In her looks and gestures, she remained her harmless, innocent, cheerful self. Inwardly she was in a crisis again, struggling fiercely, fighting to return to her parents.

She hadn't forgotten Grete Bende. Sexual matters were recalled in the strange images of the game played with four balls. Another dream told of a 'person' lying in Elli's room, 'who was quite cold'. Elli paid this person every attention, doing her best to get the cold body warmed and revived. It was, she dreamed—discreetly, but plainly—neither a he nor a she. Her sympathy for this person was striking, given her usual preoccupation with murder. It was not the dead Link. For once, it was not the dead Link. Elli was still attached to Grete and the dream made clear that not only was Grete physically separated from her; she also wished to sever her emotional ties to Grete. Elli was ashamed of this desire, but it was nonetheless alive in her. She cast it from her, just as she cast from her the dead man and the murder, revealing a close connection between the desire for severance and the deed committed against Link. There was some lingering sweetness: Elli wanted to bring Grete to life. But this was mere show, mere pretence. She went about it in quite the wrong way, trying to warm her with glowing coals. Of course the cold person ended up getting burnt. Elli wanted to have Grete Bende and, at the same time, she didn't. When the coals burnt the bed, Elli was beside herself, 'like a madwoman.' In the same way she had previously fled another, greater quandary by inflicting death.

In custody, Elli's inner life deepened. As she struggled intently, fighting symptoms that resembled a mild psychosis, a change was wrought in her that brought her closer to a reunion with her family.

Grete, however, was little affected by custody. She was much simpler, inwardly more elastic, emotionally more expansive. She remained close to her mother; that centre still held firm. Soft, jealous and sensitive, she had the odd thing to reproach Elli with. But she loved her, even in her dreams, and cherished that love. Elli was still her child who needed protecting from the bad man.

The trial, held from 12 to 16 March, was the subject of detailed and lengthy reports in all the Berlin newspapers and a good number of others. Every day brought new sensational headlines: 'Poisoners for Love', 'The Love Letters of the Lady Poisoners', 'A Curious Case'.

Elli Link sat in the dock, plain and blond, answering timidly the questions put to her. Margarete Bende, tall, with a leather belt around her slim waist, had thick, neatly waved hair and energetic features. Her mother, very upset, cried a great deal. Mrs Ella Link was charged, 'on two separate counts: with the wilful and premeditated murder of a person, namely her husband; and secondly, with aiding and abetting

Mrs Bende in her crime, namely the attempted murder of her husband Mr Bende.'

Mrs Margarete Bende was charged, 'on two separate counts: firstly, with aiding and abetting Mrs Link in her crime, namely the murder of her husband Mr Link. Secondly, with intending to kill a person, namely her husband Mr Bende, by wilful and premeditated acts which constituted the initial stages in the committal of this inchoate crime.'

Her mother, Mrs Schnürer, was charged, 'on two separate counts: with having knowledge—firstly of the intention to murder Mr Link and secondly of the intention to murder Mr Bende at such a time as those crimes were preventable—and yet neglecting to inform the authorities or alert in time the persons threatened by the crimes. Moreover, the murder of Link and a punishable attempt to murder Bende were indeed committed.'

These crimes and offences were punishable in accordance with Sections 211, 43, 49, 139 and 74 of the Criminal Code.

Twenty-one witnesses had been summoned, among them Grete's husband, the mother of the deceased, Elli's father, the Links' landlady, the chemist who had sold Elli rat poison, and the clair-voyant. Expert witnesses included the doctors who had treated Link, the pathologists who had performed the autopsy, and the chemical analyst who had examined parts of the corpse. Then there were the psychiatric experts.

To the first question put to her by the presiding judge—did she admit that she had given her husband arsenic?—Elli Link answered yes. She said that she had wanted to free herself from her husband. He had regularly come home drunk, she explained, had transferred onto her his ill-treatment of his mother, and often threatened her with a knife or rubber truncheon. He had beaten her, soiled their flat, made the most repulsive demands on her as his wife. 'Did you mean to poison your husband?'—'No. All I could think of was that he beat me, that his heart was no longer mine. Night and day, my only thought was freedom. Just to be free. I was too muddled for anything else.' When the judge expressed doubt at this—she had put a whole teaspoon of arsenic in Link's food, making him so ill that he was taken to hospital and died there; what was she thinking of when she did that?—Mrs Link replied: 'I was thinking of the maltreatment. He'd beaten me so silly I didn't know what I was doing.' When the judge pointed out that she had made no mention of the appalling things done to her in her petition for divorce, and nor were they apparent in her correspondence with Mrs Bende, Mrs Link said: 'I didn't say anything because I was so embarrassed, but I did make various statements to my lawyer.' She was encouraged by her lawyer Dr B. to speak at greater length about her husband's maltreatment of her, and the hearing was brought to a close.

The presiding judge turned to Mrs Bende. She was charged, he said, with attempting the same as Mrs Link on her own husband; she had procured a (fortunately innocuous) white powder from the clairvoyant. Mrs Bende, Margarete, replied: 'I paid several visits to Madame Feist to have the cards read, because I believed in them. At first I loved my husband because I thought he loved me in return. I married him as he was, with only the one set of clothes on his back. But our marriage turned out unhappily, because he was mixed up with criminals, and mocked and derided me for the patriotism and trust in God to which I was brought up. In the end, he threatened to stab or beat me to death and when I said: I'll barely know about it, but you will, he said: No one'll get me, I'll act the madman.' Like Elli, Margarete claimed that she was too ashamed to speak of such things in her correspondence. When confronted with compromising remarks in the letters, she tried to construe them as harmless. She was adamant that she had no bad intentions towards her husband. She had, to be sure, had her suspicions about Mrs Link, but she hadn't known that she meant to murder her husband. There in the dock, at the trial, they saw each other for the first time in months. Not knowing how they stood to one another, they exchanged searching glances, quietly pleased. Neither incriminated the other.

The third defendant, Mrs Bende's mother, wept. 'I knew nothing of all this. Old I may be, but I'd have seen to it that disaster was averted if I'd known what was afoot.'

The six hundred letters were read aloud, with breaks to question the witnesses. Chief among these was Mr Bende, a hale, burly man. He had noticed no sign of poisoning in himself. An interesting statement was made by the chemical analyst, who said he had found traces of arsenic in Bende's head hair in March. Arsenic, he explained, can be traced in the body, especially the hair and skin, even after two years. The evidence did not allow him to draw conclusions about the amount of arsenic administered. It was objected that the man had taken arsenic medicine as part of a cure; Mrs Bende and her mother insisted they had seen a prescription for it among his things. This he denied. When pressed, he admitted to certain sexual peculiarities. At the end of the second day of the trial, a number of highly compromising letters were read out in court, and the defendants, taken back to those terrible times, had a kind of breakdown. Mrs Bende fell into her mother's arms, crying, 'Dear Mother, think of your only daughter. God won't forsake us.'

Before the last letters were read, Elli's father was questioned. Much of the matter had been in his hands, though he hadn't been aware of it, and wasn't aware of it now. He was a simple, straightforward man. Elli loved him; even now, she found no fault with the decisions he had made. He stated that his daughter had complained repeatedly of her husband and his maltreatment of her. A very important witness, a colleague of the deceased, asserted with great conviction that Mr Link had been a brutal man when drunk, with a tendency to sexual excesses and a habit of boasting about them. This had obliged him—the witness—to put an end to their friendship.

When the public prosecutor called on Mr Bende again, asking him to comment on the allegedly poisoned food, there was a heated scene. Until this moment, Mrs Schnürer had kept fairly calm; now she leapt to her feet. 'You fed my daughter more poison than anyone could give you,' she flung at her son-in-law, red in the face. 'That man there poisoned my daughter, so I'm grateful to this woman [Mrs Link] for what she did. If it wasn't for her, my daughter would be dead and buried.'

The first expert witness to be called, after the chemical analyst and the two pathologists, was medical counsellor Dr Juliusberger, a dignified, widely educated man and a doctor well-versed in psychology and psychiatry. His report was extensive. The case, he said, was particularly unusual and difficult. There was no way of knowing where nature's work left off and pathology began. Mrs Link was remarkably indifferent to the ebb and flow of her emotions. Her extreme superficiality was striking. An earnest and healthy emotional reaction was not discernible in her. She was effusive in her love for her friend and in her hatred of her husband. No hint of perversion was to be found in the letters, for women would rather suffer maltreatment than reveal anything of their marital experiences to a doctor. The correspondence demonstrated a compulsion to write that could hardly be more pronounced. The letters— six hundred within five months, and often several a day—bore testimony to the pathologically heightened passion of the women's love for one another. The content of the letters combined cruelty with undisguised lust. Genuine compassion was not in evidence.

There was a delirious frenzy running through the letters that was decidedly pathological in nature. 'We can almost feel the delirium of love and hate raging in the women, especially in Mrs Link.' She had the more easily influenced nature and a childlike disposition. She was dependent on Margarete, submissive, eager to prove that her love was genuine. She did not destroy the letters, in spite of the danger they posed. This could be interpreted as the famous desire to be found out. Or one could attempt to explain it by pointing to Elli Link's feeble-mindedness. But the delirium suggested that the letters were precious to her, a kind of fetish. When did her behaviour become pathological? Mrs Link did not lack awareness; she showed no sign of delusions or hallucinations. Hers, said this prudent, sensitive and philanthropic man, was a borderline case. She could be said to be in the grip of obsessive emotions. She had a morbidly heightened temperament. It was, therefore, impossible to say that Section 51 (exemption from punishment by reason of unsoundness of mind) did not apply, but it was equally impossible to say that it did. Mrs Bende, he thought, was the stronger, more active of the two. When one examined her character and the chain of letters, there did not seem to be such extreme or abnormal tension as in Mrs Link, but there were signs of marked inferiority. Here, in his opinion, was another borderline case.

The second expert witness was medical counsellor Dr H., a broad, stout man with a thick droopy moustache. He was matter-of-fact and precise, a scientist, but a fighter too, and the man with the most practical experience in cases of this particular kind concerning relations between persons of the same sex. He arrived at the conclusion that the slow murder by poison was the result of a deep-seated hatred. The defendant Mrs Link suffered from arrested physical and mental development; Mrs Bende from hereditary imbecility. Dr H. pointed out that a writing compulsion like theirs was often accompanied by a tendency to exaggerate, so that not everything in the letters could be given credence. He saw the deep-seated hatred as caused, above all, by the women's homosexual proclivities, which made their husbands' demands particularly hard to bear, and meant that there was only one thought guiding them as they reached for one another—the fixed idea expressed by Mrs Link when she said: Just to be free. Such fanatic hatred, said Dr H., certainly diminished the women's responsibility, but in his view, neither their hatred nor their homosexual proclivities could prevent the exercise of free will as defined in Section 51. When questioned by the presiding judge, however, Dr H. conceded that Dr Juliusberger might be correct in his opinion, though for his part he did not consider the requirements for Section 51 fulfilled.

Court medical officer Dr Th. supplied his opinion: the defendant Mrs Link had acted deliberately and intentionally. Since, however, she was physically and mentally below par, her deed must be judged otherwise than if she had been perfectly sane and healthy.

The fourth expert witness, medical counsellor Dr L., rejected all mitigation. He observed that the defendant Mrs Link had never shown any want of independence in the life she led. She could not be regarded as grossly inferior; every murderer, after all, was an inferior person inasmuch as he lacked the usual inhibitions. Excess and impetuosity were typical of every passion; some were capable of a weaker, others of a stronger passion, without its being possible to speak of illness.

The senior prosecutor now asked the jurors on their benches to find Mrs Link guilty of murder and Mrs Bende of attempted murder and of being an accessory to murder. It was clear, he said, from the drawn-out nature of the killing, and the correspondence between the two women, that Mrs Link had acted deliberately. The coldness and ruthlessness evident in the letters were reason not to approve mitigating circumstances. The path of divorce had been open to the women.

It was the turn of the defence. Mrs Link's lawyer, Dr A.B., spoke first: the woman, he said, had entered marriage with high expectations, and then been maltreated by her husband in the most repugnant ways. The man's brutality eventually drove her to take up with a female. Her emotions swelled to the point of madness and she resolved to take action. Lacking all judgment and clarity of mind, she acted with imagined purpose, like a madman in his madness. The repulsive crudeness of the correspondence, the manic compulsion to write, the stashing away of the letters—all this was evidence of the strength of her delirium. Given the opinion of the first expert witness—that it was impossible to determine whether Section 51 was applicable—and the assertion of the second expert witness—that this first opinion was possibly correct—it was necessary to give the defendant the benefit of the doubt.

Mrs Bende's lawyer, Dr G., objected that the charges brought against his client were based solely on the content of the letters, which were not a reliable source of evidence. The victim of the attempted hydrochloric acid poisoning couldn't even recall the alleged attack on his life. Equally untenable was the charge of complicity brought against Mrs Schnürer, which was likewise based solely on the letters.

The jurors on the benches had listened to everything. Now twenty different verdicts were put to them. Was Mrs Link guilty of murder or manslaughter, of supplying poison, of aiding and abetting the attempted murder of Mr Bende? Was Mrs Bende guilty of aiding and abetting Mrs Link's crime, of attempted murder or manslaughter, of supplying poison? Was Mrs Schnürer guilty of failing to report the planned crime?

Inside their locked room, the jurors contemplated the strange questions that had been put to them. They were quiet and earnest men and not a few of them grew even quieter as they pondered the task before them. This was not a gathering of emotional, irascible, vengeful men; these were no warriors with swords and pelts, no medieval inquisitors. A whole apparatus had been laid out before them. The preliminary hearings had gone on for almost a year. Evidence had been produced that reached far back into the defendants' pasts. A small troop of skilled men had examined the physical and psychological state of the women, and tried to form conclusions based on their broad experience. Light had been shed on the case by the public prosecutor's speech and the statement for the defence. At the centre of all this, however, was not the crime itself, the bare murder, but almost the opposite of a crime—namely how what happened came to pass, how it was possible. There was even (this was the burden of the expert testimonies) an attempt to prove that what happened was inevitable.

The trial had left the terrain of guilt and innocence and moved onto the horribly uncertain terrain of connections, perception, insight.

Link, the deceased, had attached himself to Elli, who wasn't really fond of him. Should he be found guilty because of that? Properly speaking, he should; it was the cause and thus also the fault of what followed. Twice he had detained Elli, clearly against her will; he had tormented and maltreated her.

Elli for her part had let herself be beguiled into marriage with him. She was by nature not fully developed—frigid or sexually peculiar. Her female organs were not formed in the usual way. She rejected her husband. This excited him; it excited her. There was hatred; things ran their course.

It was the same with her friend. It was difficult—impossible—to speak of guilt as such, even of greater or lesser guilt. The jurors, shut away in their room, were faced with the necessity of finding a womb guilty, or an ovary, because it had grown this way rather than that. Really, they ought also to have had jurisdiction over Elli's father, who had led his daughter back to her husband—a man who was the epitome of bourgeois respectability. An indictment on him would have been an indictment of society.

But there was another important consideration. Something had happened—what could be done to prevent it from happening again? Intervention was called for. The court asked no questions about the part played or 'blame' incurred by Link, Elli's father or Link's mother; it singled out one fact—the murder. Wrongdoing was permitted within certain limits; if they were transgressed, it was necessary to intervene. The jurors were urged to look away from what had happened inside the circle, within the limits; they were to ignore the wider gamut of circumstances. Really, it was unreasonable to show them the whole gamut and then expect them to ignore it. But a faint echo was all they were allowed to retain—enough to go on once the facts had been established and the time had come to ask: And, are there mitigating circumstances?

After conferring for two hours, the jurors returned and pronounced their verdict: Mrs Link, they said, was guilty of deliberate but not premeditated murder with mitigating circumstances. Mrs Bende was not guilty of attempted murder, but she was guilty of aiding and abetting murder—without mitigating circumstances. The third defendant Mrs Schnürer was not guilty of complicity.

Back in his seat, the Civil Code on the bench before him, the public prosecutor proposed the maximum legal sentences for such verdicts: five years' gaol for Mrs Link and a first, erroneous sentence of eighteen months' imprisonment for Mrs Bende, which was revised to five years' penal servitude when he realised that he had overlooked the jury's refusal to grant mitigating circumstances. Mrs Bende's lawyer rose to his feet in disbelief, and pointed to the paradox of sentencing the murderess to imprisonment and her accessory to penal servitude. It was clear, he said, that the jury wouldn't have denied Mrs Bende mitigating circumstances if they'd had any notion of the severity of the punishment. The jury nodded, similarly appalled.

Mrs Bende and her mother let out screams at the public prosecutor's proposal. Their lawyer asked the court to reduce Mrs Bende's sentence to the minimum.

Elli Link was sentenced to four years' imprisonment, her friend to eighteen month's penal servitude.

In both cases, the women's brutal treatment was regarded as mitigating; the cruel nature of the deed as aggravating. For this latter reason, Mrs Link was deprived of her civil rights for six years and Mrs Bende for three years. The time spent in custody was credited towards their sentences. Mrs Bende's mother was acquitted.

The jurors, shocked by Mrs Bende's sentence and still uneasy in their minds, met after the close of the trial and filed a plea for clemency, asking for her sentence of penal servitude to be converted to a prison sentence.

The two women, who together had killed the thirty-year-old Link, were thrown into gaol and kept there year after year. They sat and counted the days and holidays, looking out for spring and autumn, and waiting. Waiting—that was their punishment. Boredom, no activity, no fulfilment. It was a true punishment. No one took their lives as they had taken Link's, but a part of their lives was taken from them. The undeniable and weighty power of society, of the state, impressed itself on them. They grew bitterer, duller, weaker. Link wasn't dead; here was the executor to his will, retaliating with loneliness and waiting and, in Elli's case, with dreams.

By punishing them in this way, the state protected

itself only feebly. It drew on none of the evidence that had been touched on during the hearing, and rather than counter the deep sense of unworthiness that had led Link to his death, it let it go on growing. There was no attempt to warn parents, teachers and priests to be vigilant and not to join together what God has put asunder. This was the work of a gardener who pulls up clumps of weeds to right and left, but can't stop the seeds from flying. When he comes to the end, he has to turn back again; behind him, everything is starting over.

Newspaper reports. In a Berlin newspaper, Dr M. wrote: 'A sex murder, a man killed out of that species of passion that drives one woman to another—those were our expectations. We were mistaken. There has been murder, wilfully committed—and yet, when one sees this plain-looking creature with her innocently blond, birdlike head, when one follows her cool, grey-blue eyes and hears her tender but quite ridiculous letters, one can only shake one's head. A childlike being who needs only tenderness, not love, encounters a man who doesn't know how to caress, who cannot love her without tormenting and maltreating her. The afflicted creature meets another woman her own age who is suffering something similar. She takes refuge in her devotion to this companion, finds a prop in her stronger character. Friendship and suppressed eros develop into sexual attachment. What more natural than that the women should form the plan of freeing themselves from such brutal men?'

In the press, the verdict was the object of a dispute governed by political and religious colour. One newspaper, the organ of a confessional party, printed the following comment: 'Once again, the jurors in Moabit Court have pronounced an astonishingly lenient verdict. The motives identified were sexual aberrations and the ensuing marital conflicts, and they were quite sufficient to explain the deed. But in their attempts to clear themselves, the woman criminals made the court listen to all kinds of stories about their maltreatment and the monstrous demands of their victim; and the jurors, to cap all their lenience, ended by filing a plea for clemency for the murderesses. In these times of general moral degeneracy, one may pity the individual criminal all one likes, but what is to become of society if crimes are so leniently judged? Would judge and jury—and even the defence—be so sure of the goodness of their hearts if they were the mourners in such cases? And is it not one purpose of punishment to deter; or have our present representatives of justice gone over in a body to the opponents of the deterrent theory?'

Expert witness Dr H., that experienced authority on homosexual love, published his own observations on the sentence—'so mild as to be unique in criminal history'—under the journal heading 'A Dangerous Verdict'. Sexual inversion did not, he said, stem from criminal intent, but from an infelicitous combination of genes. On no account did homosexual proclivities give people the right to remove obstacles by force, let alone sweep away anyone who stood in the way of their union. But this was what had happened. The jurors' verdict allowed the two young women to carry out their intention of entering into a second marriage with one another in only a few years' time. Dr H. was adamant in his refusal to see the slightest excuse for such criminal murder in the women's homosexual inclination. It was, he said, tragic that Mrs Link's father had twice led her back to Link, though she was unfit for marriage and motherhood: *a woman belongs to her husband*. But neither woman's want of intelligence—Mrs Link suffered from infantilism, a form of arrested development, and Mrs Bende from a feeble-mindedness that bordered on imbecility—was pronounced enough to preclude free will. It remained a moot point whether or not their accounts of their brutal treatment at the hands of their husbands corresponded with the facts. It seemed certain that the severely neuropathic Link loved his wife to the point of humiliation; her blankness and coldness seemed to have driven him berserk; his anger heightened her fear; her obstinacy sent him into a fury. Dr H. knew, from ample experience, to what extent woman friends of this kind were capable of poisoning their husbands' lives. One such person had once written to him: 'God help the man who buys us on the marriage market; we will cheat him of his very happiness without even meaning to.' In the case in hand, however, Elli Link took the criminal step from a metaphorical poisoning to a literal one; and our expert felt obliged to remark on the dangerous conclusions that might be drawn from her mild sentence—and, indeed, on the possible harm to the common good. He argued for the necessity of sexual education and for the reintroduction of insuperable aversion as a ground for divorce: 'A state that treats marriage as a private matter acts inconsequentially if it takes the contrary position when it comes to the dissolution of such marriage.'

In a short study of the case, K.B., a pupil of the expert witness just cited, asked whether the women's hatred was merely the result of their husbands' brutality and their homosexual love no more than a consequence of their acquired aversion to the opposite sex—or whether their homosexual emotion was innate and thus the true reason for their marital disharmony. Mrs Link claimed, credibly enough, to have had no intercourse with men before her marriage; she said she had enjoyed leading them on and then dropping them. A photograph showed her posing as a soldier; her gait and stature had some of the characteristics of the male type common to homosexual women. Mrs Bende was a less straight-forward proposition. And yet certainly her features and character displayed a great many male traits, which, taken together with the homosexual friend-ship, made innate homosexuality extremely likely.

•

The sentences of both women were carried out. Margarete Bende's marriage was dissolved due to culpability on both sides: criminal offence on her part, adultery on his.

EPILOGUE

When I look back on the whole affair it's like in the story: 'Along came the wind and tore up the tree.' I don't know what kind of a wind it was or where it came from. The whole is a carpet made up of odds and ends—cloth and silk, scraps of metal, lumps of clay. It has been darned with straw, wire and thread. In some places the pieces lie next to each other, uncon- nected. Others are held together with glue or glass. And yet there are no gaps, and everything bears the stamp of truth. It is cast in the mould of our thoughts and feelings. This is how it happened; those involved would agree. But at the same time, it isn't.

We know nothing of psychological continuity or causality, nothing of the substance of our psyche or its structures. We have to accept the facts of the case—the letters written, the acts done—and make a point of failing to interpret them in any real sense. Even if we had delved deeper here and there, we would have been none the wiser.

First of all, there are the frightfully unclear words we use to speak about such processes and relations. Wishy-washiness wherever we turn, sometimes downright childishness. The stupid, summary words to describe what goes on inside people: fondness, aversion, repugnance, love, vengefulness. A mish-mash, a muddle, designed only for simple, everyday communication. It is as if we had labelled bottles without checking the contents. Link develops a fond-ness for blithe, childlike Elli—but what changes take place in him when that happens, what brings the changes about, what course do they take, how do they end? There is a whole bundle of facts which the lazy word 'fondness' does not so much denote as overlook. The danger of such words is always that we hear them and think we understand; this prevents us from getting at the facts. No chemist would work with such impure materials. Newspaper reports and novels which tell of such lives have, by dint of repeti-tion, done much to encourage us to content ourselves with these empty words. Most interpretations of the psyche are nothing but novelistic invention.

How are we to imagine psychological connections—or, indeed, causality? We dress up the principle of causality. We take what we know and then we apply some psychology. In such cases, disorder is a knowledge superior to order.

Who is so conceited as to fancy that he knows the true driving forces behind such a crime? When I was reflecting on the three or four people involved in this affair, I felt the urge to walk the streets that they were wont to walk. I sat in the public house where the two women had met, visited the flat of one of the women, talked to her, talked to and studied others who were involved. I wasn't out for tawdry social sketches. But it was plain to me that no part of a person's life can be understood in isolation. People live in symbiosis with other people and other things. Their lives touch; they come together, grow close. That is something real and important: people's symbiosis with others and with the flats, houses, streets and squares where they live. It is, I think, a sure though obscure truth. If I single out any one person, it is as if I were to observe a leaf or the joint of a finger and then try to describe its nature and development. It can't be done: the branch and the tree, or the hand and the animal have also to be described.

What a lot is at work, what a lot goes on beyond the individual. The statistics are astonishing. The wave of suicides ebbs and flows steadily each year. There are overarching rules. From within these rules, a force emerges, an essence. The individual notices neither force nor rule, but obeys both.

How strange the simple fact: a person is young and has certain impulses; he grows older and finds his impulses changed. This happens to us all. And each of us regards his youth and love as his private affair and believes he is fulfilling his own nature. But if one person were not like another—if there weren't others like us—we wouldn't be able to understand anyone. In this truth we see a universal motor of our actions: our age in life; mankind itself. In one way or another, that motor determines the form our lives take. It is the force that drives us—nothing more.

When grim Link looks at Elli and feels fondness for her, what specific reactions take place? What brings two people together and why them rather than others? If I disregard the general course of the world, what is it in people's make-up, in their particular substances or in their organisms as a whole, that drives their urge for another person—and what is achieved by their bond and how far does it go? Chemistry has clear notions of the form and degree of interaction between substances. There is the law of mass action, the theory of affinity, and specific affinity coefficients. Reactions occur at different, precisely measured rates; substances become active under particular conditions; painstakingly studied equilibria are established. Chemical substances and their patterns of interaction are meticulously examined; all factors are determined. This is a good method. And the findings are not without relevance to the workings of the organic world. If we want to examine closely the way we act, we would do well to turn our attention to unorganised matter and the general forces of nature. For we, too, are subject to those forces—we *are* the forces that we see at work in nature, in flasks and test tubes, in us.

Zoology can help us to reveal the real motors of our actions. The large bulk of our psyche is governed by instincts. By exposing those instincts and examining them, we bring to light the driving forces behind our actions.

Then there are distant, indiscernible motors. Some human organs can be cut into without our noticing; these organs are insensible. Large tumours grow undetected in the human body. A child is bad-tempered because he hasn't had enough sleep, but he explains his temper by saying that another child hit him. In the same way, bullets can come out of the blue and hit us and change us, and we notice only the change, not the motor itself, the active force, the bullet. After that, things run their course within us. Because we react to the blow in our own way, we think we are at one with 'ourselves'.

These are the distant and indiscernible motors of our actions. They are just as they appear in Elli, who plays with men and doesn't know why she only plays. Now it is the shape of her ovary that moves her to act the way she does, now an obscure parapsychic force or set of forces, now the weave of the world. And sometimes it is not an individual, standing there before us, changing and growing, but a part of the world itself.

I have tried to demonstrate the difficulties of the case, to obliterate the impression that we understand all, or even most, of such a sizable piece of life. We understand it, on a certain level.

Elli's Handwriting

(December 1922, in custody awaiting trial.) Immediate circumstances: Elli is distracted (writing 'daß' [that] rather than 'doch' [though] in line 4, leaving letters incomplete); her downstrokes curve despondently to the right. In general, her handwriting is unintellectual, austere, functional; the lines scant and meagre. The direction of the lines is sustained, despite her preoccupation, as is the left margin; the letters are squeezed together; the writing is small: a thrifty, orderly petty bourgeois, unremarkable, with no real sense of self, though possibly obstinate and defiant (see the upper loop in 'Termin', line 3).

A reserved nature (see the formation of arcades when the letters 'n' and 'm' are joined, and in 'ich' and 'auch' [line 1]; the firm closure of the vowels 'a' and 'o'; the upside-down arch of the 'u'). The angle of writing ranges from a moderate to a pronounced leftwards slant, indicating inner coolness and a preponderance of reason over emotion, but also impulsiveness, a love of sensation and a propensity for pleasure quite without psychological equilibrium (the writing's want of clarity, its doughiness). To sum up: unrestrainedly impulsive and inflammable behind a cool, austere, reserved exterior; the whole permeated by a petty-bourgeois outlook.

Margarete's Handwriting

(Date unknown, in custody awaiting trial.) Effect of prison less marked. The handwriting altogether very different from Elli's: large, wide, leftward slanting, irregular, spilling into and generally filling the left margin. A woman with a temperament, passionate, keyed-up. Strong sense of self, fond of the limelight. No talent for making plans; so ruled by emotions that she is unable to size up or make sense of a situation. And yet no real compassion either, no tenderness (see double hooks in her 'n' and 'm'), only egoism (prevalence of clockwise loops). More open than Elli, but not significantly. Little energy or purpose; slight flagging and recovery (concavity of line 3). Greater inner unity than Elli: a flowing, connected hand;

coherence, continuity, and even adherence contrast here with Elli's volatility. Taken together with the slight flagging and want of practical ability, the large, vigorous handwriting with its air of self-assurance suggests that Margarete overcompensates, gilds the lily: she acts strong and confident but is feeble.

Elli's handwriting more troubling, more dangerous, in spite of her clean, bourgeois outlook. Margarete gregarious and weak despite her brusque, impulsive manner.

Diagrams to Show the Psychological Changes
in Elli Link, Link and Margarete Bende
November 1919 to May 1922

PHASE 1

ELLI

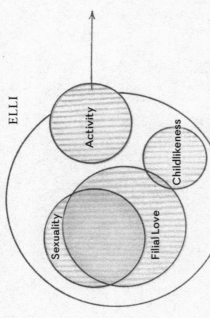

LINK

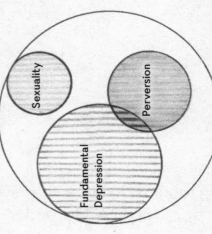

1. Old, deep-seated depression pushing at the periphery.
2. Perverse sexuality linked to fundamental depression; sadism, auto-sadism, self-destructive impulse. 2 covert but strong.
3. Normal sexuality seeking objects, relatively undeveloped.

NOVEMBER 1919: ELLI MEETS LINK

1. Sexuality almost wholly bound up with Elli's devotion to parents and family. 1 and 2 very central and strong.
2. Devotion to parents and family. 1 and 2 very central and strong.
3. Harmless, lovable nature, childlike.
4. Activity, masculine love of freedom and independence. 3 and 4 peripheral.

130

PHASE 2

ELLI

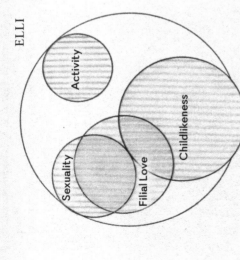

LINK

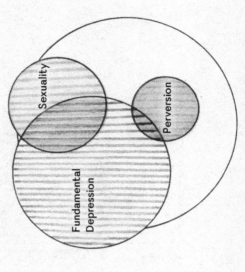

1. Fundamental depression increases under Elli's playful approach, protruding over the periphery as it demands healing, neutralisation.
2. Perverse impulses less pronounced, weaker.
3. Rise of normal sexuality invigorated by closer relations with Elli.

BEGINNING OF 1920: ELLI AND LINK GROW CLOSER

1. } Unchanged.
2. }
3. Lovable, childlike, playful nature heightened by closer relations with Link.
4. Activity withdraws.

131

PHASE 3

ELLI

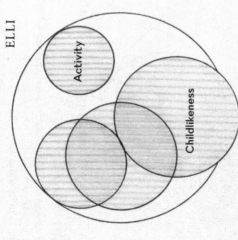

Activity

Childlikeness

1ST HALF OF 1920: ELLI AND LINK CONTINUE TO GROW CLOSER

1. } Unchanged.
2.
3. Lovable, playful nature further reinforced to attract Link.
4. Active masculine-style behaviour remains withdrawn.

LINK

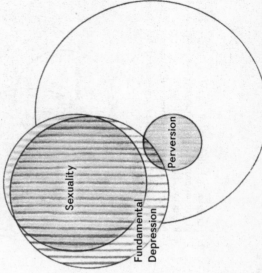

Sexuality

Fundamental Depression

Perversion

1. Fundamental depression subsides in the face of Elli's harmless, playful nature.
2. Perverse impulses further weakened.
3. Normal sexuality largely overlays Link's funda-mental depression, seeking to supplant it.

ELLI

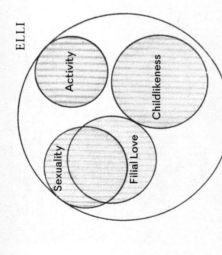

LINK

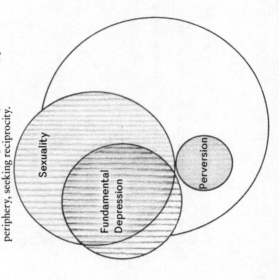

1. Fundamental depression has receded and been taken over by normal sexuality, which searches in vain for an equivalent set in Elli.
2. Perverse impulses weakened and insignificant.
3. Normal sexuality significantly increased, passes the periphery, seeking reciprocity.

END OF 1920: FIRST WEEKS OF MARRIAGE

1. } Unchanged.
2. }
3. Playfulness and attraction beat a timid retreat as Link's normal sexuality makes its attack.
4. Unchanged.

PHASE 5

ELLI

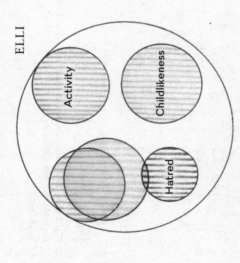

EARLY 1921: FIRST TENSIONS

1. } Unchanged.
2. }
3. Childlike playfulness withdraws and subsides.
4. Centrifugal activity increases.
5. Formation of a hate set to defend and secure the central set.

LINK

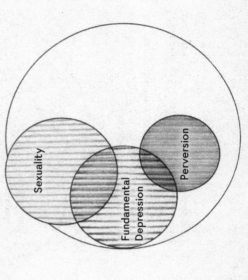

1. Fundamental depression has withdrawn inside the periphery.
2. Down below, perverse impulses increase in response to Elli's retreat.
3. Normal sexuality withdraws and weakens on finding no equivalent set, no object.

PHASE 6

ELLI

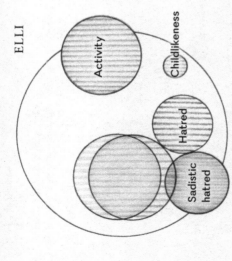

1ST QUARTER OF 1921: GROWING TENSIONS

1. } Sadistic hate set splinters off as a check to Link's sexuality.
2. } Childlike nature atrophies.
3. Activity thrusts itself over the periphery.
4. Protective hate set alongside new, active sadistic hate set.

LINK

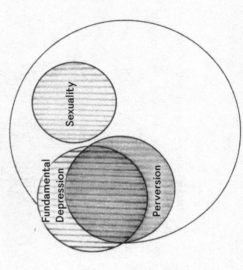

1. Fundamental depression prominent again.
2. Perverse impulses increase significantly, fuelling fundamental depression.
3. Normal sexuality continues to atrophy and subside.

ELLI   LINK

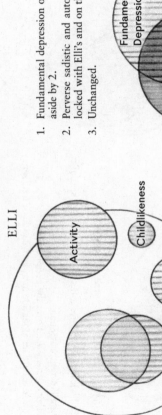

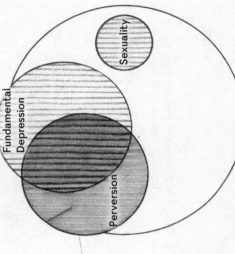

1. Fundamental depression on the surface, but edged
   aside by 2.

2. Perverse sadistic and auto-sadistic impulses inter-
   locked with Elli's and on the increase.

3. Unchanged.

2ND QUARTER OF 1921: FREQUENT ARGUMENTS,
MUTUAL HATRED; ELLI'S FIRST ESCAPE IN JUNE

1. } Unchanged.
2.

1a. Growing sadism protrudes over the periphery, strength-
    ening equivalent set in Link.

3.
4. } Unchanged.
5.

ELLI

MARGARETE BENDE

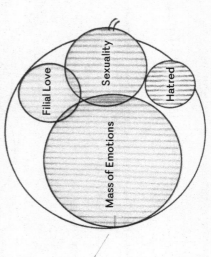

1. Nebulous, amorphous flood of emotions, lacking direction, not satisfied.
2. Devotion to mother.
3. Normal sexuality well developed, only partly fulfilled by husband.
4. Simple hatred towards husband due to unsatisfied emotions and inadequately fulfilled sexuality.

AUGUST 1921: ELLI MEETS MARGARETE BENDE

1. } Unchanged.
2. }
3. Harmless childlike nature reinforced by acquaintance with MB.

4. } Unchanged.
5. }
1a.

PHASE 9

ELLI

MARGARETE BENDE

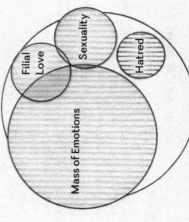

1. Nebulous mass of emotions moves towards the periphery under Elli's lure.
2. Unchanged.
3. Slackening of sexual ties to husband.
4. Unchanged.

2ND HALF OF 1921: RELATIONS UNFOLD BETWEEN THE WOMEN

1. } Unchanged.
1a.
3. Playful childlike nature continues to develop, as a lure to MB.
4. Activity, bringing out Elli's masculine side, more marked in relations with MB.
5. Unchanged.

138

ELLI

MARGARETE BENDE

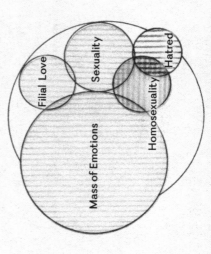

1. Amorphous mass of emotions continues in its centrifugal movement in response to Elli's lure.

2. } Unchanged.
3. }
4a.

3a. Homosexual feelings split off from sexuality and mass of emotions.

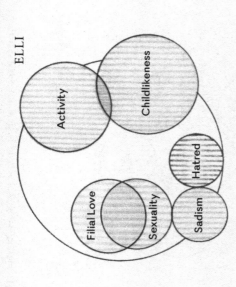

2ND HALF OF 1921: WOMEN'S RELATIONS CONTINUE TO UNFOLD

1. } Unchanged.
2. }
1a.

3. Playful, seductive impulses greatly increased.
4. Increase in active masculine behaviour.
5. Unchanged.

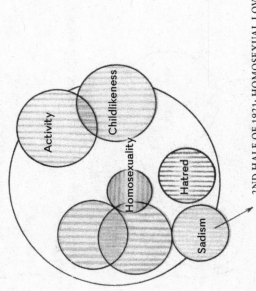

PHASE 11

ELLI

MARGARETE BENDE

Activity

Childlikeness

Homosexuality

Hatred

Sadism

Sexuality

Hatred

Filial Love

Homosexuality

Mass of Emotions

2ND HALF OF 1921: HOMOSEXUAL LOVE GROWS BETWEEN THE WOMEN

1b. Homosexual impulse splits off from more central sexuality.

3a. Newly-formed homosexual feelings drift to the periphery.

140

ELLI

MARGARETE BENDE

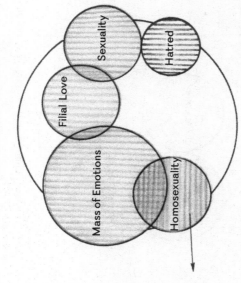

2ND HALF OF 1921: THIS LOVE CONTINUES TO GROW

1b. Split-off homosexual feelings drift to periphery, towards those of MB.

3a. MB's rapidly growing homosexual feelings push their way over the periphery, connected to and nourished by the nebulous mass of emotions.

PHASE 13

ELLI

MARGARETE BENDE

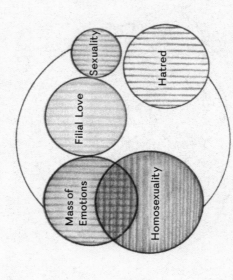

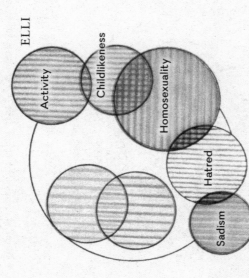

END OF 1921: THE WOMEN'S HATRED TOWARDS THEIR HUSBANDS GROWS

3. Harmless, seductive nature less pronounced.
4. Active masculine behaviour increases.
5. Hate towards Link grows.
1b. Rapid movement of homosexual feelings towards the periphery.

1. Mass of emotions diminish to the advantage of the homosexual set.
4. Hatred towards husband grows as sexual relations with Elli continue.

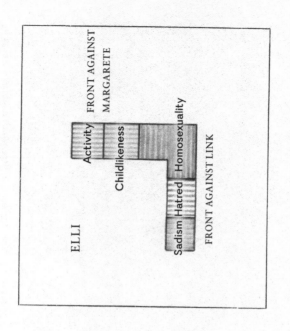

ELLI

Activity

FRONT AGAINST
MARGARETE

Childlikeness

Homosexuality

Sadism Hatred

FRONT AGAINST LINK

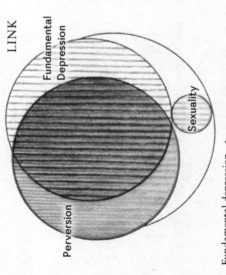

LINK

Fundamental
Depression

Sexuality

Perversion

1. Fundamental depression }
   Sadistic perversion   } grow at almost an equal rate.
   Normal sexuality atrophies.

143

MARGARETE BENDE

ELLI

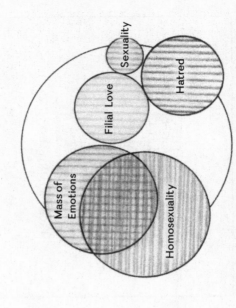

Increase in the homosexual urge which assumes a feminine hue through its contact with the mass of emotions and by contrast to Elli's masculine behaviour.[1]

The main changes here are: the considerable increase and advance of the simple hate-urge, and nascent fascination as sadistic hatred (1a) seizes the opponent. Homosexual feelings continue to grow at a moderate rate.

EARLY 1921:

ELLI'S SECOND ESCAPE, HATRED TOWARDS HER HUSBAND, HOMOSEXUAL LOVE

PHASE 15

ELLI

MARGARETE BENDE

Homosexual urge continues to grow by absorbing the amorphous mass of emotions.

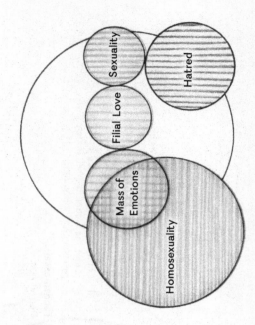

1ST QUARTER OF 1922: ELLI FORCED BACK TO LINK; POISONING BEGINS

Otherwise relatively static. The hate-urge thrust far out, provoked by the confrontation with Link's sadistic hatred. (Strong fascination, accomplishment of murder.)

LINK

The last stage of his life. Sadistic hatred turned on Elli and himself, consuming all his psychic energy. This urge coloured by his fundamental depression.

Link, chemically poisoned by Elli, is also the victim of a self-inflicted psychological poisoning.

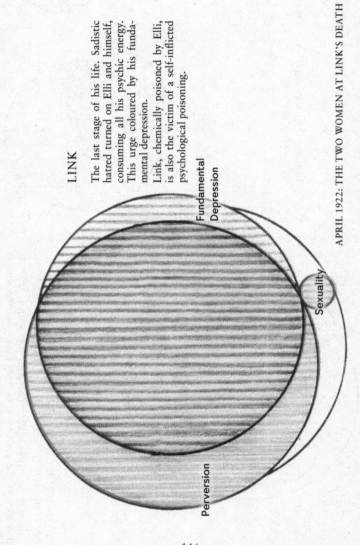

Fundamental Depression

Sexuality

Perversion

APRIL 1922: THE TWO WOMEN AT LINK'S DEATH

146

PHASE 16

ELLI

Sadistic hate-urges subside after Link's death. Simple hatred shrinks and subsides. Homosexual feelings abate following a general abatement of tension. Activity and harmless cheerfulness increase.

MARGARETE BENDE

Following Link's death MB's homosexual urge grows unchecked.

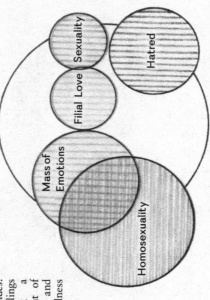

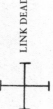

LINK DEAD

147

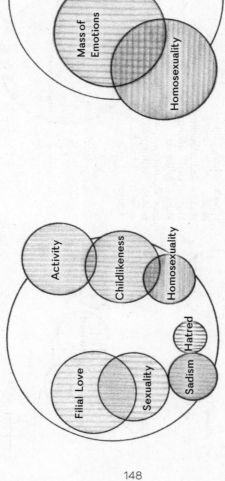

ELLI

MARGARETE BENDE

MAY 1922 AND BEYOND: THE WOMEN'S RELATIONS AFTER LINK'S DEATH

General tendency towards initial psychological state. Elli's homo-sexual urge, sadistic hatred and simple hatred shrink and subside. But her psychic energy continues to focus on these albeit small centres.

Following the changes in Elli, MB shows a slight tendency to return to her old state: a stronger heterosexual drive and a decline in her homosexual feelings and in the larger, undirected mass of emotions.

148

LINK

PREVALENCE OF THE THREE MAIN TENDENCIES IN LINK'S PSYCHE OVER THE COURSE OF THE 16 PHASES

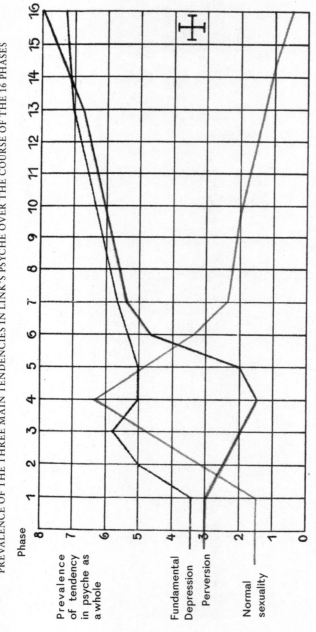

The vertical axis (1-8) shows the prevalence of the tendencies. The horizontal axis (1-16) shows the changes in prevalence over the course of the 16 phases (1-16).

Mrs Nebbe and Mrs Klein
by Joseph Roth

Mrs Nebbe and Mrs Klein are up before the court for murder by poisoning. Mrs Klein killed her husband; Mrs Nebbe did not succeed. Mrs Nebbe was the active party and, possibly unawares, the goader; Mrs Klein was the goaded, the weaker, the 'bondwoman'. The stronger failed in her attempt; the weaker successfully poisoned her husband. She was armed with more zeal, more fire, more obsession.

The force of Mrs Nebbe was at work within her, raised to a higher power by her 'bondwoman's' passion.

Yet however strange this 'sensational trial' and however odd the two women, their marriages and lives are typical of the petty-bourgeois circles from which they hail. This gives the trial particular social and psychological significance. In the great, cruel city, a thousand marital tragedies are played out daily; only coincidence prevents crimes from being committed or conceals those that are—and the horror takes its toll in silence and the law knows nothing of what goes on.

From a psychological point of view, the murderesses are interesting because they offer proof of the highly complex processes at work in these primitive women we think we know so well when we encounter them on trains and in shops and on the street. Perversity and cunning, mystery and entanglement are not necessarily the result of highbrow decadence or the nervous sensitivity that comes from continued breeding; rather, they are the result of innate unnatural emotional storms, the conditions for which are everywhere, in all of us—in the 'simple' peasant soul and the 'sophisticated' organism of the intellectual. Those at the trial who were mature enough to shut out the thrilling and lascivious side of things and draw a lesson from what happened will have arrived at the conclusion that the angels and devils in us have equal powers and equal chances of victory; and that the unnatural leanings that were present in the women from the start—and are perhaps present in us all—were bred by their observance of the social rule.

Thousands of women suffer in marriage as Mrs Klein unquestionably did. They suffer at the hands of sadistic males whose weak brutality so often conceals itself in the gargantuan bulk of a berserker. It is a cruel trick of nature to house weaklings in colossal bodies to which they are not equal. Their minds are too feeble for their excessive muscular power, and nature's useless gift finds its release only in brutality, which is the heroism of cowards.

Thousands of women suffer and say nothing. In the cases of Nebbe and Klein, however, the cruelty of man awakened an inclination for the opposite of the male—for the female. This inclination grew into a passion—yet it was not this alone that led to the crime, but the women's knowledge of the unlawful and forbidden nature of their love. It was not with an act of passion, but with an act of taboo, a 'sin', that they began their descent into murder.

Their particular species of murder, moreover—murder by poison—seems by common consent to be regarded as especially morally objectionable. The newspapers repeat the banal, unoriginal and shabby opinion that poison is an insidious weapon, a woman's weapon, a weapon of 'stealthy revenge'. Such indignation at the method of murder recalls the protests so often heard during the war against enemy acts that were in violation of international law, though they are a necessary consequence of war. People were appalled at the use of dumdum bullets, but gladly forgave hand grenades. It says something for the keenness of the human conscience, but hardly speaks for the logic of human reason that even atrocities are expected to be humane. Poisoning someone is, in the end, no more or less cowardly than jumping out at him and striking him dead with an axe. There is no humane method of murder; even the 'electric execution' in America is not humane. Mrs Klein and Mrs Nebbe turned to murder out of love for one another; their hatred of their husbands was only a secondary motive. Doing away with the men was merely a means to an end, the end itself being to fulfil their desire. They had to kill cleverly so as to be free to exercise their love. They had to use poison because it was the least likely to betray them.

This method, of course, resulted in protracted deceit and a constant comedy. But there is no truth in the prevailing opinion that long dissimulation weighs heavy on a murderer. The human soul knows enduring lust, abiding passion, chronic desire—and they are neither better nor worse than the acute varieties. Hatred feeds off its own strength; the longer it lasts, the fiercer it becomes, and each act it spawns is committed 'in the heat of the moment', even the long and carefully prepared. For preparation itself is an integral part of the *'crime passionnel'*.

Perhaps the murder would never have come about if the women had found help and counsel close at hand. The true misfortune of the classes which we are in the unconscionable habit of referring to as 'lower' is not so much their ignorance or lack of humaneness as their total dependence on society and custom. Mrs Klein's old father clung to the traditional prejudice that a daughter, once happily married off, no longer belongs in her father's house, but to her husband. He was beguiled by the prevailing notion that a husband is lord over his wife, even when his power is undeserved. And Mrs Klein, who is so staunch in her belief in moral principles that even now she spurns her only means of rescue and would rather confess to murder than to a lesbian relationship—Mrs Klein feared and suffered and hated until the hatred filled her soul and bubbled over, rousing unnatural desire and murderous cravings, cruelty, dissimulation, destruction and self-destruction.

Berliner Börsen-Courier, 17 March 1923
Originally published in Joseph Roth, *Werke*, ed. Klaus Westermann, Cologne, 1989, vol. 1, pp. 952–954

A Criminal Couple: A Tale of
Two Unhappy Marriages
by Robert Musil

These last days in Berlin have seen the end of a trial that rightly attracted a good deal of attention and revealed conflicts which one would wish had received attention before they came to court. A Mrs Elli K. was sentenced to four years' imprisonment for the murder of her husband; her friend, Mrs N., who was acquitted of attempting the same on her own husband, was sentenced to eighteen months' penal servitude for aiding and abetting her. The sentencing is in itself noteworthy: aiding and abetting was punished with a shorter term but a more severe penalty than murder. We cannot know which weighs heavier on the psyche—the length of punishment or the type—but this uncertainty reflects the psychological nature of the crime.

Elli K., the daughter of simple people, married at a young age a master craftsman, and fled back to her parents after the first weeks of marriage, horror-stricken for reasons that remain unknown because shame prevented her from talking about them, even in the most critical situations. Compelled to rely on vague conjecture, we can only assume one of two causes: either brutal and probably perverse sexual behaviour on the part of the man, or exceptional sensitivity due to inverted feeling in the young woman. One would have thought that in a civilised society—and given the importance we continue to attach to the family in our social order—the woman's parents could have stepped in with some sound advice and help. But no. Outraged father orders immediate return to husband. Parental authority, as so often, perverted in its course!

Elli K. returns, only to flee again a few months later, this time to friends; a petition for divorce is filed, but has to be withdrawn, because the harried woman is in no state to confide to a lawyer the horrors she has been through, or perhaps only imagined—for under the intimidating pressure suffered in her parents' house, even minor injuries may have developed into major psychological trauma. So the marriage goes on, in all its horror, hatefulness and violence.

Now comes the second twist which, like all that follows, is so typical that it might have been taken from a scientific treatise. Elli K. meets Mrs N., who is likewise unhappily wed to a brute of a man whom she married, evidently somewhat rashly, after the war. A liaison develops between the women; this would seem to suggest a strong lesbian element to Elli's marital aversion, but it is also possible that it takes her friendship with Mrs N. to arouse in her those slight homosexual leanings that are present in almost all of us. As so often in such cases, the swelling emotion is not satisfied by daily contact, and an exchange of passionate letters begins, of which six hundred alone will be submitted to the court. The women decide to free themselves from their husbands by killing the monsters. Their chosen method is poison, administered in imperceptibly small daily doses. It is plain that Mrs N. has the leading role in this criminal liaison; after all, it is not she who commits the crime, but Elli K.!

For experience has taught us that in such relationships, the stronger never does the deed himself, but talks the weaker into doing it—often with some initial resistance. He does not act in cold blood; it is not that he intends to let his friend do the deed alone. It is simply that the more susceptible of the two is the one more easily swayed by mutual suggestion. Thus Elli K. is the victim of her friend Mrs N., although she commits the more severe crime. The sentencing always poses difficulties in such cases, and the legal studies that struggle to reconcile the inviolability of the law with the fragility of psychological distinctions are not without their comic side. It is, moreover, probably fair to assume that both women suffered from a degree of psychopathic inferiority—though this need not mean that they were socially inferior!

There is a book by the Italian sociologist Scipio Sighele, entitled *Le crime à deux* in the French translation from 1910, which contains hundreds of such cases, all of which follow an almost identical pattern. I quote, by way of example, two extracts from letters written by a woman to a younger man she was trying to inveigle into murdering her husband: 'Tuesday is the anniversary of the first month of our love; I send you a flower to mark the day; I will do everything in my power to belong to you alone [she mixed poison into her husband's food!]. Oh! how I long to be free! I suppose the stuff [dynamite, which he was to put in her husband's shotgun!] is very hard to get hold of?' Another extract: 'He was sick yesterday; I think God must be beginning His work.' The emotional language of these passages reveals to us not only how the noble feeling of love is transformed into a crime, but also how a thought that is outwardly criminal can feel inwardly indistinguishable from a noble feeling of love. In cases of this kind we should ask with particular urgency what portion of blame society bears for letting things come to this pass. J. St. Mill says that an energetic criminal may harbour more evil than a weak, good man, but that he also harbours more seeds of good.

20 March 1923

Originally published in Robert Musil, *Gesammelte Werke*, ed. Adolf Frisé, Hamburg, 1978, vol. 7, pp. 669–671